Alice in Charge

Books by Phyllis Reynolds Naylor

Shiloh Books

Shiloh
Shiloh Season
Saving Shiloh

The Alice Books

Starting with Alice
Alice in Blunderland
Lovingly Alice
The Agony of Alice
Alice in Rapture, Sort of
Reluctantly Alice
All But Alice
Alice in April
Alice In-Between
Alice the Brave
Alice in Lace
Outrageously Alice
Achingly Alice
Alice on the Outside
The Grooming of Alice
Alice Alone
Simply Alice
Patiently Alice
Including Alice
Alice on Her Way
Alice in the Know
Dangerously Alice
Almost Alice
Intensely Alice

The Bernie Magruder Books

*Bernie Magruder and the Case
    of the Big Stink*
*Bernie Magruder and the
    Disappearing Bodies*
*Bernie Magruder and the
    Haunted Hotel*
*Bernie Magruder and the
    Drive-thru Funeral Parlor*
*Bernie Magruder and the Bus
    Station Blowup*
*Bernie Magruder and the
    Pirate's Treasure*
*Bernie Magruder and the
    Parachute Peril*
*Bernie Magruder and the Bats
    in the Belfry*

The Cat Pack Books

The Grand Escape
The Healing of Texas Jake
Carlotta's Kittens
Polo's Mother

The York Trilogy

Shadows on the Wall
Faces in the Water
Footprints at the Window

The Witch Books

Witch's Sister
Witch Water
The Witch Herself
The Witch's Eye
Witch Weed
The Witch Returns

Picture Books

King of the Playground
The Boy with the Helium Head
*Old Sadie and the Christmas
    Bear*
Keeping a Christmas Secret
Ducks Disappearing
I Can't Take You Anywhere

Alice in Charge

PHYLLIS REYNOLDS NAYLOR

Atheneum Books for Young Readers
New York • London • Toronto • Sydney

ATHENEUM BOOKS FOR YOUNG READERS
An imprint of Simon & Schuster Children's Publishing Division
1230 Avenue of the Americas, New York, New York 10020

This book is a work of fiction. Any references to historical
events, real people, or real locales are used fictitiously. Other
names, characters, places, and incidents are products of the
author's imagination, and any resemblance to actual events or
locales or persons, living or dead, is entirely coincidental.

ATHENEUM BOOKS FOR YOUNG READERS is a
registered trademark of Simon & Schuster, Inc.
For information about special discounts for bulk purchases,
please contact Simon & Schuster Special Sales at
1-866-506-1949 or business@simonandschuster.com.
The Simon & Schuster Speakers Bureau can bring authors
to your live event. For more information or to book an event,
contact the Simon & Schuster Speakers Bureau at
1-866-248-3049 or visit our website
at www.simonspeakers.com.
Book design by Ann Zeak
The text for this book is set in Berkeley Old Style.
Manufactured in the United States of America
First Edition
2 4 6 8 10 9 7 5 3 1
Library of Congress Cataloging-in-Publication Data
Naylor, Phyllis Reynolds.
Alice in charge / Phyllis Reynolds Naylor. — 1st ed.
p. cm.
Summary: Along with the usual concerns of senior year in high
school, Alice faces some very difficult situations, including
vandalism by a group of neo-Nazis and a friend's confession that
a teacher has been taking advantage of her.
ISBN 978-1-4169-7552-6
[1. High schools—Fiction. 2. Schools—Fiction.
3. Neo-nazism—Fiction. 4. Race relations—Fiction.
5. College choice—Fiction. 6. Family life—Maryland—Fiction.
7. Maryland—Fiction.] I. Title.
PZ7.N24Akdm 2010
[Fic]—dc22 2010000798

To Victoria

Contents

Alice in Charge

Starting Over

It was impossible to start school without remembering him.

Some kids, of course, had been on vacation when it happened and hadn't seen the news in the paper. Some hadn't even known Mark Stedmeister.

But we'd known him. We'd laughed with him, danced with him, argued with him, swum with him, and then . . . said our good-byes to him when he was buried.

There was the usual safety assembly the first day of school. But the principal opened it with announcements of the two deaths over the summer: a girl who drowned at a family picnic, and Mark, killed in a traffic accident. Mr. Beck asked for two minutes of silence to remember them, and then a guy from band played "Amazing Grace" on the trumpet.

Gwen and Pam and Liz and I held hands during the playing, marveling that we had any tears left after the last awful weeks and the day Liz had phoned me, crying, "He was just sitting there, Alice! He wasn't doing *anything*! And a truck ran into him from behind."

It helps to have friends. When you can spread the sadness around, there's a little less, somehow, for each person to bear. As we left the auditorium later, teachers handed out plastic bracelets we could wear for the day—blue for Mark, yellow for the freshman who had drowned—and as we went from class to class, we'd look for the blue bracelets and lock eyes for a moment.

"So how did it go today?" Sylvia asked when she got home that afternoon. And without waiting for an answer, she gave me a long hug.

"Different," I said, when we disentangled. "It will always seem different without Mark around."

"I know," she said. "But life does have a way of filling that empty space, whether you want it to or not."

She was right about that. Lester's twenty-fifth birthday, for one. I'd bought him a tie from the Melody Inn. The pattern was little brown figures against a bright yellow background, and if you studied them closely, you saw they were tiny eighth notes forming a grid. I could tell by Lester's expression that he liked it.

"Good choice, Al!" he said, obviously surprised at my excellent taste. "So how's it going? First day of your last year of high school, huh?"

"No, Les, you're supposed to say, 'This is the first day of the rest of your life,'" I told him.

"Oh. Well then, this is the first minute of the first hour of the first day of the rest of your life. Even more exciting."

We did the usual birthday thing: Lester's favorite meal—steak and potatoes—the cake, the candles, the ice cream. After Dad asked him how his master's thesis was coming and they had a long discussion, Les asked if I had any ideas for feature articles I'd be doing for *The Edge*.

"Maybe 'The Secret Lives of Brothers'?" I suggested.

"Boring. Eat, sleep, study. Definitely boring," he said.

From her end of the table, Sylvia paused a moment as she gathered up the dessert plates. "Weren't you working on a special tribute to Mark?" she asked. Now that I was features editor of our school paper, everyone had suggestions.

"I am, but it just hasn't jelled yet," I said. "I want it to be special. Right now I've got other stuff to do, and I haven't even started my college applications."

"First priority," Dad said.

"Yeah, right," I told him. "Do you realize that every teacher seems to think *his* subject comes first? It's the truth! 'Could anything be more important than learning to express yourselves?' our English teacher says. 'Hold in those stomach muscles, girls,' says the gym teacher. 'If you take only one thing with you when you leave high school, it's the importance of posture.' And Miss Ames says she doesn't care what else is on our plate, the articles for *The Edge* positively have to be in on time. Yada yada yada."

"Wait till college, kiddo. Wait till grad school," said Lester.

"I don't want to hear it!" I wailed. "Each day I think, 'If I can just make it through this one . . .' Whoever said you could slide through your senior year was insane."

Lester looked at Sylvia. "Aren't you glad you're not teaching high school?" he asked. "All this moaning and groaning?"

Sylvia laughed. "Give the girl a break, Les. Feature articles are the most interesting part of a newspaper. She's got a big job this year."

"Hmmm," said Lester. "Maybe she *should* do an article on brothers. 'My Bro, the Stud.' 'Life with a Philosophy Major: The Secret Genius of Les McKinley.'"

"You wish," I said.

• • •

In addition to thinking about articles for *The Edge* and all my other assignments, I was thinking about Patrick. About the phone conversation we'd had the night before. Patrick's at the University of Chicago now, and with both of us still raw after Mark's funeral, we've been checking in with each other more often. He wants to know how I'm doing, how our friends are handling things, and I ask how he's coping, away from everyone back home.

"Mostly by keeping busy," Patrick had said. "And thinking about you."

"I miss you, Patrick," I'd told him.

"I miss *you*. Lots," he'd answered. "But remember, this is your senior year. Don't give up anything just because I'm not there."

"What does that mean?" I'd asked.

I'd known what he was saying, though. We'd had that conversation before. Going out with other people, he meant, and I knew he was right—Patrick is so reasonable, so practical, so . . . *Patrick*. I didn't want *him* to be lonely either. But I didn't feel very reasonable inside, and it was hard imagining Patrick with someone else.

"We both know how we feel about each other," he'd said.

Did we? I don't think either of us had said the words *I love you*. We'd never said we were dating exclusively. With nearly seven hundred miles between us now, some choices, we knew, had already been made. What we did know was that we were special to each other.

I thought of my visit to his campus over the summer. I thought of the bench by Botany Pond. Patrick's kisses, his arms, his hands. . . . It was hard imagining myself with someone else too, but—as he'd said—it was my senior year.

"I know," I'd told him, and we'd said our long good nights.

In my group of best girlfriends—Pamela, Liz, and Gwen—I was the closest to having a steady boyfriend. Dark-haired Liz had been going out with Keeno a lot, but nothing definite. Gwen was seeing a guy we'd met over the summer when we'd volunteered for a week at a soup kitchen, and Pamela wasn't going out with anyone at present. "Breathing fresh air" was the way she put it.

There was a lot to think about. With our parents worrying over banks and mortgages and retirement funds, college seemed like a bigger hurdle than it had before. And some colleges were more concerned with grades than with SAT scores, so seniors couldn't just slide through their last year, especially the first semester.

"Where are you going to apply?" I asked Liz. "Gwen's already made up her mind. She's going to sail right through the University of Maryland and enter their medical school. I think it's some sort of scholarship worked out with the National Institutes of Health."

"She *should* get a scholarship—all these summers she's been interning at the NIH," said Liz. "I don't know—I think I want a really small liberal arts college, like Bennington up in Vermont."

We were sitting around Elizabeth's porch watching her little brother blow soap bubbles at us. Nathan was perched on the railing, giggling each time we reached out to grab one.

"Sure you want a small college?" asked Pamela, absently examining her toes, feet propped on the wicker coffee table. Her nails were perfectly trimmed, polished in shell white. "It *sounds* nice and cozy, but everyone knows your business, and you've got all these little cliques to deal with."

"Where are you going to apply?" Liz asked her.

"It's gotta be New York, that much I know. One of their theater arts schools, maybe. Somebody told me about City College, and someone else recommended the American Academy of Dramatic Arts. I doubt I could get into Cornell, but they've got a good drama department. Where are you going to apply, Alice?"

I shrugged. "Mrs. Bailey recommends Maryland because they've got a good graduate program in counseling, and that's where she got her degree.

But a couple of guys from church really like the University of North Carolina at Chapel Hill. . . ."

"That's a good school," said Liz.

". . . And I've heard good things about William and Mary."

"Virginia?" asked Liz.

"Yes. Williamsburg. I was thinking I could visit both on the same trip."

"You could always go to Bennington with me," said Liz.

"Clear up in Vermont? Where it *really* snows?"

"It's not Colorado."

Just then a soap bubble came drifting past my face, and I snapped at it like a dog. Nathan screeched with laughter.

What I didn't tell my friends was that lately I'd been getting a sort of panicky, homesick, lonely feeling whenever I thought about leaving for college—coming "home" at night to a dorm room. To a roommate I may not even like. A roommate the complete opposite of me, perhaps. I don't know when I first started feeling this way—Mark's funeral? Dad's worries about investments and the store? But at college there would be no stepmom to talk with across the table, no Dad to give me a bear hug, no brother to stop by with an account of his latest adventure.

It was crazy! Hadn't I always looked forward to being on my own? Didn't I want that no-curfew life? I'd been away before—the school trip to New York, for example. I'd been a counselor at summer camp. And yet . . . All my friends had been there, and my friends were like family. At college I'd be with strangers. I'd be a stranger to them. And no matter how I tried to reason myself out of it, the homesickness was there in my chest, and it thumped painfully whenever college came to mind, which was often. I didn't want to chicken out and choose Bennington just to be with Liz or Maryland just to room with Gwen. Still . . .

Nathan tumbled off the railing at that point and skinned his knee. The soap solution spilled all over the porch, he was howling, and we got up to help. That put an end to the conversation for the time being, and time was what I needed to work things through.

The school newspaper, though, kept me busy. Our staff had to stay on top of everything. We were the first to know how we'd be celebrating Spirit Week, because we had to publish it. We had to know when dances would be held, when games were scheduled, which faculty member had retired and which teachers were new. We were supposed to announce new clubs, student trips, projects, protests. . . . We were the school's barometer, and in our staff meetings we tried to get a sense of things before they happened.

We were also trying something different this semester. Because of our newspaper's growing reputation and the number of students who'd signed up to work on *The Edge*, we'd been given a larger room on the main floor, instead of the small one we'd been using for years. Here we had two long tables for layout instead of one. Four computers instead of two. And on the suggestion of Phil Adler—our news editor/editor in chief—we were going to try publishing an eight-page newspaper every week instead of a sixteen-page biweekly edition.

We wanted to be even more timely. And because the printer's schedule sometimes held up our paper for a day, we were going to aim for Thursday publication. Then, if there was a snafu, students would still get their copies by Friday and know what was going on over the weekend.

"I've got reservations about this, but it's worth a try," Miss Ames, our faculty sponsor, told us. "I know you've doubled your number of report-ers, and you've got an A team and a B team so that not everyone works on each issue. But you four editors are going to have to work *every* week. That means most Mondays, Tuesdays, and Wednesdays after school. Can you can swing it?"

We said we could. Phil and I and Tim Moss, the new sports editor (and Pamela's old boy-friend), and Sam Mayer, the photography editor (and one of my old boyfriends), all wagged our woolly heads and said, yes, of course, no problem, we're on it. All completely insane, of course.

It will keep me from thinking so much about missing Patrick, I thought. But each day that passed brought me that much closer to D-day— decision time—and what I was going to do about college.

It was through *The Edge* that I found out about Student Jury. Modeled after some counties where student juries meet in city hall, ours would be a lot simpler, according to Mr. Beck. He decided that if more decisions and penalties were handed down by students themselves—overseen, of course, by a faculty member—maybe Mr. Gephardt, our vice principal, could have more time for his other responsibilities, and maybe the offenders would feel that the penalties were more fair. Students guilty of some minor infraction would be referred to the jury and would be sentenced by their peers.

The Edge agreed to run a front-page story on it, and I found out that I'd been recommended by the faculty to serve on the jury.

"No way!" I told Gwen. I had assignments to do. Articles to write. If anyone should serve on it, she should.

"So what have you got so far on your résumé?" was her answer.

"For what? College?"

"Well, not the Marines!" We were undressing for gym, and she pulled a pair of wrinkled gym shorts over her cotton underwear. "Extracurricular stuff, school activities, community service. You've got features editor of the paper, Drama Club, the Gay/Straight Alliance, some volunteer hours, camp counselor . . . What else?"

"I need more?"

"It can't hurt. You've got heavy competition." Gwen slid a gray T-shirt down over her brown arms and dropped her shoes in the locker. "Student Jury—dealing with kids with problems—might look pretty impressive, especially if you're going into counseling."

I gave a small whimper. "I told you the paper's coming out weekly, didn't I? I'm still working for Dad on Saturdays. I've got—"

"And William and Mary is going to care?"

Gwen's impossibly practical. "You and Patrick would make a good couple," I told her.

"Yeah, but I've got Austin," she said, and gave me a smug smile.

Later I whimpered some more to Liz and Pamela, but they were on Gwen's side.

"I've heard you need to put anything you can think of on your résumé," said Pamela. "I'm so glad you guys talked me into trying out for *Guys and Dolls* last spring. If I was sure I could get a part in the next production, I'd even jump the gun and include that."

They won. I told Mr. Gephardt I'd serve on Student Jury for at least one semester.

"Glad to have you on board," he said, as though we were sailing out to sea.

Maybe, like Patrick, I was trying to "stay busy" too. Maybe it made a good defense against going out with other guys. But I *did* keep busy, and whenever I felt my mind drifting to Mark, out of sadness, or to Patrick, out of longing, or to college, out of panic, I wondered if I could somehow use my own musings as a springboard for a feature article: "When Life Dumps a Load," "Long Distance Dating: Does It Work?" "Facing College: The Panic and the Pleasure"—something like that.

Amy Sheldon had been transferred from special ed in our sophomore year and had struggled to go mainstream ever since. I'm not sure what grade she was in. I think she was repeating her junior year.

It's hard to describe Amy, because we've never quite decided what's different about her. She walks with a slight tilt forward and is undersized for her age. Her facial features are nonsymmetrical, but it's mostly her directness that stands out—a childlike stare when she talks with you about the first thing on her mind . . . and the way she speaks in non sequiturs, as though she's never really a part of the conversation, and I suppose in some ways she never is. Somehow she has always managed to attach herself to me, and there have been times when I felt as though I had a puppy following along at my heels.

The same day I said yes to Student Jury, Amy caught up with me after school. I had taken a couple of things from my locker, ready to go to the newsroom, when Amy appeared at my elbow.

"I've got to wait till Mom comes for me at four because she had a dentist appointment and then I'm getting a new bra," she said.

"Hey! Big time!" I said. "What color are you going to get?"

She smiled in anticipation. "I wanted red or black, but Mom said 'I don't think so.' She said I could have white or blue or pink."

"Well, those are pretty too," I told her. I realized I'd closed my locker without taking out my jacket and opened it again.

"I went from a thirty-two A to a thirty-two B, and a year ago I didn't wear any bra at all. I hate panty hose. Do you ever wear panty hose?"

"Not if I can help it," I said.

"I wouldn't want to wear a rubber bath mat around me," Amy said.

I blinked. *"What?"*

"Grandma Roth—she's my mother's mother—used to wear a Playtex girdle when she was my age. She said it was like wrapping a rubber bath mat around her. She even had to wear it when it was hot. I hate summer, do you? Am I asking too many questions?"

I tried to dismiss her comment with a quick smile but saw how eagerly she waited for an answer. "Well, sometimes you do ask a lot."

"My dad says if you don't ask questions, how do you learn anything? You know why I like to ask questions?"

"Um . . . why?" It seemed she was going to follow me all the way down the hall.

"Because people talk to me then. Most of the time, anyway. Most people don't come up to me and start a conversation, so I have to start one, and Dad says the best way to start a conversation is to ask a question. And you know what?"

If I felt lonely just thinking about college, I imagined how it must feel to be Amy, to be lonely most of the time. "What?" I asked, slowing a little to give her my full concentration.

"If somebody just answers and walks away, or doesn't answer at all, you know what I say? 'Have a nice day!'"

I could barely look at her. "That's the perfect response, Amy," I said. "You just keep asking all the questions you want."

•••

I was deep in thought, my eyes on the window, as Phil went over our next issue. We could give free copies to all the stores surrounding the school, he said, just to be part of the community and maybe help persuade them to buy ads; the art department had suggested we use sketches occasionally, drawn by our art students, to illustrate some of our articles; and we still needed one more roving reporter in order to have an equal number for each class. A few reporters from last year had graduated, and some had dropped out for another activity.

I suddenly came to life. "I'd like to suggest Amy Sheldon," I said, and the sound of it surprised even me.

There was total silence, except for one girl's shocked *"Amy?"* Then, embarrassed, she said, "Are you sure she can handle it?"

"I don't know," I said honestly. "But I'd like to give her a try. She's good at asking questions."

There was a low murmur of laughter. "Boy, *is* she! Remember when she went around asking other girls if they'd started their periods?" someone said.

"Now, *there's* a good opener," said Tim. More laughter.

"Everybody likes to be asked questions about themselves, and if she bombs, we don't have to print it."

Silence. Then Phil said, "Can you offer her a temporary assignment—so she won't get her hopes up?"

"Sure, I could do that." I waited. The lack of enthusiasm was overwhelming.

I watched Phil. I'd met him last year when I joined the Gay/Straight Alliance in support of my friends Lori and Leslie. He'd been a tall, gangly roving reporter before, but now that we were seniors, he was head honcho and looked the part. It was weird, in a way, that all the people who had run the paper before us were in college, and now we were the ones making the decisions.

"Okay," Phil said at last. "We'll give it a try. But have a practice session with her first, huh?"

"Of course," I said, and realized I'd added still one more thing to my to-do list.

"In the same spirit," Miss Ames said, "I'd like to suggest an article now and then by Daniel Bul Dau." When a lot of us looked blank, she added, "He's here from Sudan—you may have seen him around school. He's eighteen, and his family is being sponsored by a local charity. I think he could write some short pieces—or longer ones, if he likes—on how he's adapting to American life, his take on American culture, what you have to overcome in being a refugee . . . whatever he wants to write about. He's quite fluent in English."

We were all okay with that. More than okay.

"Feature article, right?" Phil said, looking at me, meaning this was my contact to make.

"Give me his name and homeroom, and I'll take care of it," I offered, and wondered if there would be any time left in my schedule for sleep.

Daniel Bul Dau had skin as dark as a chestnut, wide-spaced eyes that were full of either wonder or amusement or both, and a tall, slim build with unusually long legs. On Tuesday he smiled all the while I was talking with him about the newspaper and the article we wanted him to write.

"What am I to say?" he asked.

"Anything you want. I think kids would be especially interested in what you like about the United States and what you don't. Your experiences, frustrations. Tell us about life in Sudan and what you miss. Whatever you'd like us to know. I'll give you my cell phone number if you have any questions."

"I will write it for you," he said, and his wide smile never changed.

Gwen and Pam and Liz and I were talking about teachers over lunch. Specifically male teachers. Who was hot, who was not, who was married, who was not. We were trying to figure out Dennis Granger, who was subbing for an English teacher on maternity leave.

"Married," Pamela guessed. "I wouldn't say he's hot, but he's sort of handsome."

"Not as good-looking as Stedman in physics," said Gwen.

"I caught him looking at my breasts last week," said Liz.

"Stedman?"

"No, Granger."

"Kincaid looks at butts," said Pamela.

"Kincaid? He's as nearsighted as a person can be!" I said.

"That's why he has to really study you from every angle," said Pamela just as Dennis Granger approached our table and looked at us quizzically as we tried to hide our smiles. I think he deduced we were talking about guys and jokingly ambled around our table as though trying to eavesdrop on the conversation. He leaned way over us, pretending to mooch a chip or a pickle from somebody's tray, his arm sliding across one of our shoulders. We broke into laughter the moment he was gone.

"The best teacher I ever had was Mr. Everett in eighth grade," Liz said when we recovered. "I wish there were more like him."

Pamela gave her a look. "Yeah, you were in love with him, remember?"

"Crushing, maybe," said Liz.

"One of the best teachers I ever had was Sylvia," I told them.

"And then your dad goes and marries her," said Liz.

"Well, she couldn't be my teacher forever. I liked Mr. Everett, too. But I totally loved Mrs. Plotkin. Remember sixth grade? I was so awful to her at first and did everything I could to be expelled from her class. She just really cared about her students."

"That's why I want to be a teacher," said Liz.

"You'll make a great one," I told her.

"And you'll make a great counselor," said Liz.

Pamela rolled her eyes. "While you two are saving the world, I'll be working for a top ad agency in New York, and you can come up on weekends."

"With or without boyfriends?" asked Liz.

"Depends on the boyfriends," said Pamela.

"I thought you were going to a theater arts school," said Gwen.

Pamela gave an anguished sigh. "I just don't know what to do. I used to think I'd like fashion designing, but I've pretty much given that up. So it's between theater and advertising. I'm thinking maybe I'll try a theater arts school for a year to see if they think I have talent. If I don't measure up, I'll leave and go for a business degree somewhere. Of course, then I'd be a year behind everyone else."

"Pamela, in college that doesn't matter," said Gwen. "Go for it."

Liz looked wistfully around the group. "You'll be off doing medical research, of course," she said to Gwen. "Remember how we used to think we'd all go to the same college, sleep in the same dorm, get married the same summer, maybe? Help raise each other's kids?"

"I'm not having kids," said Pamela.

Gwen chuckled. "Hold that thought," she said. "We'll check in with each other five years from now and see what's happening."

2

Marshaling the Troops

I caught up with Amy after seventh period when I recognized her somewhat lopsided walk at the end of the hall. I sped up. From outside, I could hear the buses arriving.

"Amy?"

She looked around, then stopped and turned. Her face lit up like a Pepsi sign. "Alice!"

"Your hair looks nice," I told her, and it did. "How are things going?"

"I curl my hair on Tuesdays and Thursdays. Oh, and on Sundays," she said.

"Are you taking a bus home?"

"Yeah."

"Well, I have a favor to ask, and I could drive you. We can talk about it in the car," I said.

She stared at me in delight, like a kid being offered a marshmallow cookie. "Sure! Anytime! You just name it and I'll do it! Except sometimes

MARSHALING THE TROOPS • 23

I'm slow on account of I'm slow, but that doesn't mean I can't do something. I have to stop by my locker."

"Okay. Why don't I meet you at the statue in about five minutes," I suggested.

"If I'm not there in five minutes, I'll be there in six minutes, maybe, on account of I'm slow," she said.

"I'll wait, don't worry."

"Because if you don't wait for me and I miss the bus, I can't get home. Then I have to call my dad, and he has to leave an important meeting or something to come get me and he says, 'Amy, I am not pleased.'"

"I'll be there, Amy. The statue near the entrance."

"Yeah. The man on the toilet."

I laughed. "That's *The Thinker*, Amy. By Rodin."

She laughed too. "I knew that, but he still looks like he's on the toilet."

Amy's a small girl with a nice figure. Tiny waist. She sat in the passenger seat with her knees together, shoulders straight, a bit like a soldier at attention.

"Is this your own car?" she asked as I turned the key in the ignition.

"No, it's Dad's. Sometimes I drive him to work, and Sylvia picks him up and brings him home."

"If you ever asked me to drive this car, I couldn't," Amy said.

I smiled. "I wasn't going to ask you that. I wanted to talk to you about—"

". . . because I'd get the brake and the gas pedals mixed up, Dad says."

"Don't worry. I can't let anyone else—"

". . . Or maybe the windshield wipers and the lights."

This is a huge mistake, I thought, but I took the plunge. "I have a question to ask you."

She grew quiet.

"You read *The Edge*, don't you?"

"Of course! I'm up to seventh level now, and Mrs. Bailey says I'm doing great."

"Good! So here's the thing. We're missing a roving reporter for the issue after next and wondered if you'd like to try out."

Amy turned sideways and stared at me. Then she faced forward again. "No," she said.

"Really?" I glanced over. "Why not?"

"Tryouts make people laugh," she answered. No non sequiturs there.

"What I meant was, we'll give you a question to ask, and then you ask it to maybe five or six people and write down their answers. We'll choose the best ones and help edit them. And if we use yours in the newspaper, we'll print your name, as reporter."

Amy shook her head. "I don't have a car. I can't drive anywhere, and when I'm twenty-one, I probably still won't have a car."

"You don't need one, Amy." I turned off East-West Highway and looked for her street. "You just ask kids at school. You can choose anyone you like, and you won't have to leave the building."

"And you'll help me?"

"Absolutely. I won't go around with you to ask the question, though. You'll have to do that on your own, but we'll need to practice first. We could do it before or after school."

Amy sat motionless for a few seconds when I stopped at her house. Then she opened the door. "Maybe," she said. "I'll talk to Dad."

She called me that night, excited to the point of giddy. I almost told her the deal was off, but I couldn't back out now.

"Dad will drive me in tomorrow, Alice, and I'll be there at seven o'clock and you just tell me where, because if I don't write it down, I'll probably forget. . . ."

She was waiting for me when I got to the newsroom the next morning at six fifty-five.

"I'm here, Alice!" she said, her notebook and pen at the ready.

"Great!"

We sat down across from each other at one of the long tables.

"We're going to do a feature article on sleep," I told her. "One of our senior reporters is going to write the main story about how students don't get all the sleep they need. We want you to ask five students how many hours of sleep they get at night. Write down exactly what they say and be sure to get their names—spell them correctly too—and what class they're in: freshman, sopho-more, junior, or senior."

I could tell by Amy's expression that these were too many instructions, all coming at her at once.

"Let's practice," I said. "Pretend you're sitting across from me in the cafeteria. What are you going to say?"

Amy shook her head. "Nobody sits across from me. Not usually."

"Okay. Let's say you came up to me in the hall. What are you going to ask?"

"How much sleep do you get at night?"

"That's it, but first you need to explain why you're asking. Something like, 'Hi, I'm a reporter for our school paper, and I'd like to ask you a question.'"

"But I'm really not."

"Not . . . a reporter?"

She nodded.

"Well, for this one week, you are. Let's try it."

Amy took a deep breath and stared at me unblinking. "Hi, I'm a reporter, and I'm going to ask you a question."

"Very good, but you need to mention our paper and then *ask* if you might ask them a question."

"That's too many questions."

I felt both my confidence in her and my patience waning. "It's the polite thing to do, though, because maybe this isn't a good time for them to be stopped and questioned. Maybe they're in a hurry. Try it again and mention *The Edge*."

Amy's eyes drifted to the wall, and her voice sounded like the automated message you get on an answering machine: "Hi, I'm a reporter for *The Edge*, and . . . do you care if I ask you a question?"

"That's pretty good, Amy."

"Now what?"

"Ask the question."

"Oh. Do you sleep at night?"

"How *much* sleep do you get at night? And it would probably be better if you said, 'On average, how much sleep, or how many hours of sleep, do you get at night?' Can you remember all that?"

Amy gave a big sigh and bent over her notebook, laboriously writing down the whole sentence, then reading it aloud: "Hi. I'm a reporter for *The Edge*, and could I ask you a question?"

"Excellent!" I said.

"On the average, how much sleep do you get at night?"

"Well, I guess I average about five and a half hours. Maybe six," I told her.

Amy stared at me. "I go to bed at nine thirty. I get eight and a half hours."

"No, Amy, you're supposed to be writing down my answer. You don't need to tell people how much sleep *you* get. *You're* the one asking the question."

She bent over her notebook again. When she had finished, I said, "Wanna try it once more?"

Another deep breath, and she faced me again: "I'm a reporter for *The Edge*, and could I ask you a question?"

I nodded and smiled to let her know we were rehearsing: "I guess so," I said. "What's the question?"

She paused and glanced down at her notebook. "On average, how much sleep do you get at night?"

"I suppose about five and a half hours. Maybe six."

She bent over her notebook and wrote it down. "Okay, thanks," she said.

"Don't walk away yet, Amy," I said. "Ask my name and what class I'm in."

"I already know that," she said. "You're a senior."

"Reporters always have to double-check. Ask even if you know."

"What's your name and what class are you in?" Amy asked.

"Alice McKinley, senior," I said.

She beamed.

"Don't forget to thank them, Amy," I instructed.

"Thank you, Alice. I'm a reporter now!" she said delightedly.

I only wished I felt that confident.

There was a short assembly on Friday to talk up Spirit Week, the last week of September. Gwen, as a member of the Student Council, brought down the house by coming onstage in a wet suit and flippers. Her left foot kept stepping on her right flipper, almost tripping her, and we screamed with laughter.

When she took the microphone, Gwen told us she was getting in the mood for Beach Day, the first day of Spirit Week. The other days would be announced in *The Edge*.

Then she turned the program over to Mr. Gephardt, who told us what great sports teams we had this year and that they'd be introduced at the pep rally at the end of Spirit Week.

Then he spent the rest of the time talking about the Student Jury system we were now ready to inaugurate at our school, explaining in detail how certain kinds of misconduct would be handled as usual by him and Mr. Beck, but some students might find themselves facing a jury of their peers. The judgments made by the jury would be respected by the faculty, and the penalties it imposed would be enforced. It was time, he said, for students to participate not only in the victories and celebrations of our school, but in reinforcing the values and conduct in keeping with our reputation and traditions.

I'll admit that the main thing I brought away from that assembly was the memory of Gwen in those flippers, but her hair was remarkable too. Her friend Yolanda had given it an elaborate cornrow design in four large triangles, two braids on either side sweeping around her head and joined in back.

"Seriously," I asked her later, "how long did it take her to do your hair? It's amazing."

"Six and a half hours," Gwen confessed. "But I did my history assignment while I was sitting there."

● ● ●

I don't know how Gwen does it. The school year had only begun, and already I was questioning how much I could handle. Saturdays I worked for Dad at the Melody Inn. The only morning I could sleep in was Sunday, and sometimes I wanted to hang out with the high school discussion group at church.

"I wish I could clone myself," I said one evening after dinner. "I could take on Mondays, Wednesdays, and Fridays, and my clone could do Tuesdays, Thursdays, and Saturdays."

"I'm glad you're the one who brought this up, because Sylvia and I have been worried about you," said Dad. "Sometimes your light's still on at one in the morning. I hate to see you studying so late."

"Ha! I'd like to know what time *Gwen* turns out her light," I said. "I don't do half the stuff she does."

"You've got to apply to colleges, Al. The only one you've visited so far is the University of Chicago."

"I've got a list," I said. *A mental list, anyway.*

"You do?"

"You don't have to worry. Les is taking me around," I lied.

Now both Dad and Sylvia looked surprised. "When? Which colleges?" Dad asked.

You know how in the movies the phone rings at exactly the right moment to further the plot? I'm not kidding, the phone rang right then, and I almost fell out of my chair getting up. I reached for it on the wall. Les usually calls about this time when he calls at all, and yes, right on cue, it was Les. Am I lucky or am I lucky?

"Hey, Al!" he said. "Dad there?"

"Yeah. It sure is, Les!" I said brightly. "Let me get the list."

"Huh?" said Lester.

"Are you at the apartment?" I asked.

"Yes. What's going on? I just want to ask Dad a question."

"I'll call you right back," I said, and hung up.

"It was Les. We're making plans," I told Dad and Sylvia, and zipped upstairs for my cell phone.

I was still breathless when I punched in his number.

"What the heck?" he said when he answered.

"Les, you've got to help me!" I pleaded. "I need this huge favor. What are you doing the third weekend in October?"

"Al, I don't even know what I'm doing *this* weekend," he said.

"Well, that Friday is an in-service day for teachers, so I've got the whole weekend to visit colleges."

"Now, listen . . ."

"It's making me crazy, and I don't have enough time—enough brain cells—to do all I'm supposed to be doing. I have to get my applications out, and Dad thinks I should look at some colleges first, and—"

"*What* colleges? Why can't Dad or Sylvia take you?"

"Les, you *know* how they are! They'll ask me to talk to financial advisers and find out the number of books in the libraries and—"

"So?"

"How many colleges did *you* visit, Lester?"

"I'm not your role model."

"Les, just take me around to a couple, okay? I told them we had it all planned."

"Alice!"

"*Please!* I already know the University of Maryland, and I just want to see a few more."

"What colleges are you talking about? Southern California, I suppose?"

"Of course not. I was thinking about the University of North Carolina—"

"Chapel Hill? That's the whole weekend right there!"

"But we can do it, Les. I looked at a map. After that, William and Mary and George Mason."

"William and Mary is in Williamsburg, Al. It's not just across the Potomac River."

"Listen, Les. Do you remember how I traded that fur bikini last Christmas for the granny gown you gave a girlfriend by mistake? Do you remember when Liz and Pamela and I bailed you out of jail?"

I heard a deep sigh. "Can we do this in two days, Al, and be home by Sunday afternoon so I can watch the Redskins with my buddies?"

"I promise!" I said gratefully. "We can start out at four in the morning if you want."

"But *you've* got to do all the preliminary stuff—set up the appointments, arrange for tours, bring a list of questions. I'm just the driver, understand?"

"You're worse than Dad."

"I mean it, Al."

"Okay. I'll even help drive."

"No, thanks."

"Promise you'll put it on your calendar?"

He sighed again. "It's on. I'm writing it now in big black letters. Underlined. Exclamation point. Now tell Dad I've got a tax question."

"Thank you, Les," I said. "You're the best!"

And I rushed downstairs to tell Dad and Sylvia that—like I said—it was all arranged. Sometimes life *is* just like the movies.

3

Student Jury

I was one of five jury members, all juniors and seniors, who'd been selected by the faculty. My friend, Lori Haynes, a member of the Gay/Straight Alliance, was on it; so was Darien Schweitzer, a guy from the debate team; Kirk Manning, a friend of Patrick's from band; and Murray Hardesty, the junior class treasurer.

We'd been through an orientation session with Mr. Gephardt. We weren't pretending to be lawyers, he'd told us. We weren't police officers or judges. Our job was to listen to a complaint brought in against a student, get his take on it, and decide on the solution or the penalty. We selected Darien as jury foreman for these sessions that would take place about once or twice a month on Wednesdays after school. One of our teachers, on a rotating basis, would be present each time as faculty adviser.

Our first "offender of the month," as Darien

put it, was led into the faculty conference room by the school secretary, Betty Free, followed by one of the custodians. We five jurors were seated around the long polished table, notepads and pens in front of us, unsmiling.

But this didn't prompt the sophomore coming through the door to adjust his cocky walk or wipe the smirk from his face. I was thinking how hard it is to keep from making first impressions, because the smirk and the careless way he walked made me want to say, *Nail him. Case closed.*

Mr. Gephardt and two teachers observed our first session.

"Would you give the jury your name?" Darien asked him.

The kid cast him a somewhat disgusted glance and mumbled, "You already got my name."

"For the record," Mrs. Free said, seating herself at the end of the table with her laptop.

"Kenny Johnson," the defendant said.

"You've been called before the Student Jury for making a mess—several of them—in the cafeteria, despite warnings from Mr. Garcia to stop," Darien read.

"Hey, there were other guys. It wasn't just me," said Kenny.

"Please remain silent until the charge is read," Mr. Gephardt instructed from the side of the room.

Kenny shrugged and slowly faced forward again. Darien went on reading the charge: "On two occasions last week and one the week before, you were seen dumping food on the table, throwing food, smearing mustard on someone's T-shirt . . ."

Kenny grinned a little. We didn't respond.

"Mr. Garcia, do you want to add anything?" Mr. Gephardt asked the angry custodian.

"I tell him to stop, he laughs. I make him clean up the table once, and then I see he greased all the chairs," Mr. Garcia complained.

Kenny suppressed a chuckle.

"I got no time for this! I got whole cafeteria to clean by three o'clock." Mr. Garcia turned and stared hard at Kenny, who only lowered his head, grinning at the floor.

"Okay, Kenny. Your turn," said Darien.

"Aw, it's only in fun, man. I didn't hurt anyone. The other kids were laughing, and it was Joe's idea to butter the chairs. So I cleaned them up! What's the big deal?" Kenny said.

"Big deal for me!" Mr. Garcia said heatedly. "You got time, maybe, but I don't have time to watch you all day, see what you do next."

Mr. Gephardt broke in, not allowing Kenny more time than he deserved. "Any questions from the jury?"

"How old are you?" Lori asked Kenny.

"Fifteen," Kenny answered.

"You bring your lunch or buy it?" asked Kirk.

"Buy it, mostly."

"Your money or your parents'?" Kirk wanted to know.

Kenny had to think about that a few seconds. "My dad's, I guess."

We nodded to each other that we'd heard enough, and the secretary escorted Kenny back to the library across the hall while we discussed it. The custodian was excused. Mr. Gephardt and the teachers let us debate it among ourselves.

"What do you think?" asked Darien. He's a round-faced, somewhat pudgy guy, with a radio announcer's voice, who could run for any office on his smile alone. But he wasn't smiling now.

"Ten years, maximum security," Murray quipped. "It's obvious he thinks he's funny."

"Mr. Garcia has the whole cafeteria to do single-handed, with community groups using it some evenings," Lori said. "All he needs is a joker like Kenny."

"What about the other kids who he said were in on it too?" I asked.

"Mr. Garcia says it's always Kenny who starts it, from what he's observed," Mr. Gephardt said.

"And I've seen one instance of it myself," a teacher put in. "I was there the day he was 'buttering the chairs,' as he put it."

We deliberated for about five minutes, then Darien went across the hall to tell Mrs. Free we were ready. She led Kenny back in.

His shoulders were a little less relaxed, we noticed, as he stood at one end of our table, his smile a little less fixed.

Darien read the verdict: "The jury has decided that Kenny Johnson's problem seems to be that he's forgotten how old he is and thinks he's still five. So we've decided he needs the job of a man for a week to keep his focus on being fifteen. We recommend five days' detention in the cafeteria during the lunch hour. He'll be responsible for seeing that all garbage is removed from the trays, all trash bags are tied up and hauled out to the Dumpster. He'll wash down the tables, wipe off the chairs, mop the floor, or do any other job assigned to him by Mr. Garcia. If he doesn't do his work well or does it discourteously, he'll repeat his detention the following week." He looked at Kenny. "Any questions?"

This time the defendant wasn't smiling. "Yeah, when do I eat?"

"That's your problem," said Darien. "Excused."

After Kenny left, Mr. Gephardt nodded his approval. "I'll tell security to keep an eye on him, make sure he gets there every day," he said.

The only problem with bimonthly jury duty

was that our newspaper deadline is also on Wednesdays. I got back to the newsroom in time to do a short write-up and get it on the computer in the space Phil had allowed. We decided we'd report each Student Jury case so students would be aware of how the panel worked, describing the incident and the penalty assigned, but we wouldn't name the defendant. Enough for Kenny to be embarrassed doing cleanup in front of his friends, and they'd guess soon enough.

It was a mistake to send Amy around asking questions. The feature story would focus on how much homework teachers assign and how much sleep, or how little, we get because of it. Amy came by the newsroom over lunch on Thursday, and I could tell she was down.

"Nobody makes any sense," she said, looking at her notebook. "And they won't even give me their names."

I hadn't expected this much trouble. Usually kids are eager to get their names in *The Edge*. "You asked how much sleep they got at night?"

She nodded and read off the five replies: "'Who wants to know?' 'You're a *reporter* now?' 'Yeah, right.' 'Don't bother me.' 'Later, maybe.'"

I felt anger rising inside me as I imagined her humiliation. But it was largely my fault. "You know what, Amy? You just need an official badge," I said, my mind racing. I opened the drawer where we keep plastic holders for name tags when we send reporters to a board of education hearing. I printed out a badge in Times New Roman bold typeface and slid it in the holder. But I realized when I pinned it on her that even this might not be enough. Did I really want her to fail twice?

"Listen, Amy," I said. "I just want you to ask five teachers the same question. We'll include them in the article so kids will realize they're not the only ones up late at night."

She did it. By the close of school on Friday, Amy had five quotes from teachers, and after I'd typed them into the computer, I showed her the printout of what the article would look like. The teachers, of course, had answered Amy's question politely, and Miss Ames was pleased with the way the whole thing was coming together. Following the feature article, "Who Stays Up Late and Why?" with a byline from a senior reporter, were the two questionnaires:

HOW MUCH SLEEP DO YOU GET AT NIGHT? (STUDENTS)
—Josh Logan, roving reporter, senior

Courtney Brookings: "Six, usually. Five, if there's an exam."

Sherry Hines: "You've got to be kidding. Four to five hours, if I'm lucky."

Todd Gambi: "Depends who I'm sleeping with."

Emma Herringer: "Last night I was up until two."

Lei Song: "Five hours. Weekends, I sleep all day."

HOW MUCH SLEEP DO YOU GET AT NIGHT? (TEACHERS) —Amy Sheldon, roving reporter, junior

Oscar Evans (history): "The eleven o'clock news is my cutoff time."

Luis Cardello (Spanish): "Four to five hours, don't ask me how."

Dennis Granger (sub): "I never go to bed till I've watched *The Tonight Show*."

Jennifer Smythe (biology): "From midnight on."

Roy Peters (phys ed): "Sleep? What's that?"

"Amy, you did a great job!" I told her. "How did you get such short answers?"

"I told them there wasn't a lot of space," Amy said, obviously thrilled at seeing her name on copy. "I remembered how it looked before."

Now that she'd been seen around school wearing a badge, saw that her name was in the paper, she'd be more accepted, I told myself.

"Should we tell her she can keep the job?" I asked Phil.

"Try her a few more times—see how it goes," he said.

Gwen, Pamela, Liz, and I sat in Starbucks Sunday afternoon discussing life, or "getting a life," as Pamela put it.

"I've never had so much homework!" she complained. "I thought senior year was supposed to be a breeze. If I go to a theater arts school, what does any of this matter? Grades, I mean."

"They show you can think—that you can complete an assignment, you're not a quitter," said Gwen.

"What if you got a part in a historical play and didn't know anything about England? Or about how it was during the Depression?" asked Liz.

"Ugh," said Pamela, skimming the whipped cream off her latte and eating it with a spoon. "That's not exactly what I had in mind."

"What *did* you have in mind?" I asked.

"I don't know. TV. Sitcoms. I haven't decided yet. I still think about design sometimes. Or advertising. I'm all over the map."

"So be a travel agent!" Liz joked. "You'll travel the world and see exotic places. *Meanwhile*, who's going to the Homecoming Dance? Why don't we all go together?"

"Aren't you inviting Keeno?" asked Gwen. "I'm bringing Austin."

"I did, and he said he could get his mom's SUV for the evening if he pays for the gas. Can pack in eight people."

"Make it seven," I said. "I'm not going with anyone."

"Make it six," said Pamela. "I'm not either."

Gwen looked us over. "What's wrong with you guys?"

"I just want it to be fun and easy," said Pamela. "If I meet someone at the dance, fine, but I'm not looking right now."

Gwen turned to me.

"Ditto," I said. "Patrick told me not to give up dances and stuff just because he's not here. Fine. I'm not giving up the Homecoming Dance. I'm just not inviting another guy, that's all."

"And we're wearing . . . ?" asked Gwen.

"The tightest jeans we've got," said Pamela.

4

An Unexpected Invitation

Monday: Beach Day; Tuesday: Twin Day; Wednesday: Garage Band Day; Thursday: Tacky Day; Friday: Time-Warp Day.

Our school did it up big this year. Each class was assigned a hallway to decorate for Spirit Week with some particular theme: Between the four classes, we chose Arabian Nights, Disney World, Chicago Mobsters, and the Cosmos. It felt sort of schizoid to walk past Mickey Mouse at one corner and then find yourself on Mars.

I liked Tacky Day best—liked going to the Gay/Straight Alliance meeting after school in an old green polyester sweater with pill balls all over it and a red, white, and blue scarf around my neck. Waist down, I wore baggy brown sweatpants and some gold ballerina slippers with pink butterfly buckles.

The guy I sat next to just had his shirt on inside out.

"That's *tacky*?" I teased, but he looked a little embarrassed, and I was sorry because he was new to the group. A junior, I think.

"I'm Alice McKinley," I said. "I only look this bad part of the time."

He gave me a little smile. "Curtis Butler," he said. And then, glancing around the group, "How many members?"

"It varies," I said. "A dozen. Sometimes more."

"Just wanted to see what it's all about," he said.

"Tolerance and acceptance—that whatever you are, you're welcome here," I told him.

Lori and Leslie arrived in camouflage-type jackets, plaid pants, and purple socks rolled down around their ankles. Each person who came in seemed to look more tacky than the one before, and we especially cheered and clapped when Mr. Morrison, our faculty sponsor, showed up in striped pants that rode up as far as his rib cage and a sweater vest over a yellowed nylon shirt.

Some of the members rehearsed the crazy skit they'd be doing at the pep assembly the next day, and we laughed and applauded as three guys, dressed as girls in hockey uniforms, and three girls, wearing football uniforms, came face-to-face on a practice field and didn't know what to make of each other. After circling uncertainly, the football girls tackled the hockey boys, who swung at them with their sticks, and they all ended up in a heap on the floor, where everybody disentangled, hugged, and sang a syrupy rendition of "People" to hoots of laughter.

I'm not sure what kind of impression we made on Curtis, except that we have a good time at our meetings.

The fall sports pep rally was probably the best ever, and I was glad that Phil was going to do the write-up on it because I just wanted to enjoy it without taking notes. It's mostly run by students. The junior and senior class presidents acted as hosts, introducing the various sports and dance teams, and the clubs on campus that performed the skits. The senior girls did their traditional dance, and I did okay, even though I'd missed a few of the six a.m. rehearsals. But the skit by the GSA got a huge laugh and loud applause, and I felt even better about that.

For the first time the principal didn't come onstage to announce our annual blood drive. Instead, the Health Occupations Students of America Club performed a mock operation with an IV full of bright red "blood," to remind people of the current shortage, and told the audience how we could go about giving blood on a scheduled day.

The rally ended with bleacher mania, led by

the cheerleaders—a competition to see which class cheered the loudest. Liz and I had put coins and rice in plastic bottles for noisemakers, and Pamela brought a whistle. Justin Collier brought a cowbell. Our ears were ringing when we left the gym, but every person was smiling.

The game that night was something to celebrate because it was the first time in three years that we won our first home game. The bleachers went nuts. None of my best friends had gone out for cheerleading—Pamela thought about it once—but we knew the cheers and started a few of our own when we got the chance.

The best part, though, was the old senior tradition of streakers at half time. All week long the school had buzzed with speculation about which guys were going to do it, and just after the marching band had strutted its stuff, two seniors dropped their clothes and went racing across the field as we shrieked and cheered them on.

But it was the next day that really got to me. Dad let me have the afternoon off at the Melody Inn so I could watch the homecoming parade. It was the music, I guess, that reminded me of how much I was missing Patrick. It was nothing we shared—I can't even sing. But each year when there was a band concert or a game, Patrick was there, playing the drums. When the school put on its spring musical, Patrick was there in the orchestra, doing percussion.

The way he held his back so straight. The way his feet moved, absolutely in step. The way he held the sticks. The way the chin strap on his hat creased his jaw. The little smile he'd give me as he marched past, letting me know he saw me, even though his eyes didn't move left or right.

Now, watching the band go by, there were parts in the marches where the drummer played solo for a couple of measures, and I wanted it to be Patrick playing those parts, not the short guy out there in the street, and I could feel tears welling up momentarily.

Justin and Jill—surprise! surprise!—had been elected homecoming king and queen, and they rode the float along with the full homecoming court. It was a gorgeous October day. Everyone in Maryland, it seemed, was outside in the red-orange of this autumn afternoon, taking photos as the band passed, including Sam, our *Edge* photographer. I knew I'd treasure the next issue of the newspaper because this would be my last homecoming parade in Silver Spring. My last Homecoming Dance. Senior year: the last of everything.

• • •

"Wow!" Sylvia said, rolling her eyes as I ate a little supper at the kitchen counter. "Can you sit down in those pants?"

I laughed and swallowed a last bite of cheese. "They're brand new, but I should have them broken in by the end of the evening. You like?"

"They're terrific! Too bad that Patrick—" She stopped suddenly, but I picked up where she'd left off.

". . . isn't here to take me to the dance, right? I know. But a lot of kids are going solo. Having a carful helps."

Keeno phoned to say he was running late—his mom just got home with the SUV—so as soon as I heard him pull up in front, I grabbed my jacket and ran out.

Music was playing inside the car, and I slid in beside Gwen and Austin, the guy with the dreadlocks and the linebacker shoulders. Liz was up front with Keeno, and Pamela was in the very back. The inside of the car smelled great—Pantene shampoo and Abercrombie's Fierce. I was glad to see Gwen in heels, because I wasn't sure of the footwear.

The people who weren't at the dance were as obvious as the ones who were. Mark. Patrick . . . Patrick on an October night in Chicago. Roaming the campus alone? Sitting on a bench by Botany Pond, thinking of me?

I have to say we seniors looked great. Hot. *Finally* our faces were almost blemish-free. Maybe a spot or two on the forehead or a makeup-covered zit on the chin. But looking around at all the other girls in their slim pants and sparkly tees, we looked rather magnificent. We all had breasts; we all had waists. Had learned to wear eyeliner expertly, abandoning the old raccoon look.

And the guys! How had they grown so tall in just one summer? The guy who used to be called Mr. Zits now had beard shadow all over his face, like some movie star. We were top of the heap, king of the hill. This was our time, and we immediately began to dance.

The sophomore Student Council members had decorated the gym with streamers intertwined to form a canopy over the dance floor, and there were balloons everywhere. One of the football team's blockers served as DJ. I was glad to see Amy Sheldon happily tagging along with two other girls, and she waved to me as they circled the gym.

"Best turnout yet!" said Phil as he came over to dance with me. "Sam says he's got some great photos. We'll try to get them in the next issue."

"We're going to be working our butts off to get a paper out every week, Phil," I said, thinking of Sam and all he had to do.

"Well, we'll see how it goes," he said. "Ames is really pleased at the reviews we got last year. Some of the graduates even want their parents to send the paper to them at college."

I danced with Darien, too, and then I ran into Pamela and Gwen, who were teaching Daniel Bul Dau to dance.

It was a riot, the way he towered over them, but he seemed to be enjoying himself, taking his mistakes with good humor.

"To dance by myself, I do very fine. When I dance with you, we have four feet to get in the way of each other," he explained, laughing, when Pamela tried to teach him the basics of slow dancing.

He held her so far away from his body that I could have walked between them. But Daniel so wanted to fit in. By the end of the evening he'd perfected the box step and had managed to dance with three of us. His smile made him look as though he'd conquered the world.

"What kind of dances do you do in Sudan?" Austin asked him when we gathered at the refreshment table.

Daniel laughed again. "Not very much like this one. And not with girls."

"Really?" said Pamela. "Who do you dance with?"

"All of the men dance together, but they

are not touching like this. They dance, and the women watch them."

"Aha!" said Gwen.

"But I never danced because I was too young. My brother is twenty-three, and he did not dance either. We were small when we had to leave our village."

"Well, you're doing great," Pamela told him. "We'll even give your brother a lesson if he wants one."

For me, it was a sort of bittersweet evening— the first year of school since we'd moved to Silver Spring that I wasn't in a class with either Patrick or Mark. Like life was going to go on same as before—it was interesting and happy—except that there was a big hole in it, and a lot of the time I felt I was just watching other people live their lives. Every so often I'd feel that rush of loneliness— sort of a panicky, sinking feeling—and wondered if Amy Sheldon felt this way a lot. It wasn't that I was here without a boyfriend necessarily; I had fun with my female friends. It was just that some- body important in my life was missing. This was my senior year! I wanted Patrick now, I wanted him here, and I felt envious of Jill and Justin.

"What in the world are you thinking about?" Liz asked when she found me standing in a door- way holding a cup of Sprite. "You look like the Girl Without a Country."

"A violin without a string," I said. "A pebble without a beach. A nest without an egg. A—"

"Omigod," said Liz. "A pity party if I ever heard one."

And then it was over, and I felt better.

I went to church with Dad and Sylvia the next morning. The senior high group meets over in Chalice House during the second service, and it's usually like a discussion group, focusing on some general problem in society or with ourselves. If anyone's home from college, he knows this is a place to catch up with friends and trade news and gossip, and sometimes we head for the Tastee Diner afterward for waffles.

I didn't see any of the kids who had left for college, but I did recognize one of the girls from "Our Whole Lives"—a series of classes Dad signed me up for in my sophomore year. I'd met Emily at the first awkward session of that group, and she was the one who had suggested we might just crawl out the window and escape.

"Hey, how are you?" Emily asked. "Haven't seen you for a long time."

"Just catching up on life," I said. She goes to a different school, and we compared teachers and classes.

Bert Soams, one of the instructors of "Our Whole Lives," was leading senior discussions now, and he'd written a single sentence on the board. Eventually the conversation drifted to that:

At the moment of your conception, four hundred million spermatozoa were racing for the egg, but only one of them fertilized it, and that one became you.

It was pretty awesome when you thought about it, and it didn't take long to start a discussion. If any one of those other sperm had got there first, we'd all have been different people. Maybe the opposite sex. I mean, think of the odds. What a gamble! What a coincidence! What a miracle! All of us sitting in that room were miracles.

I told Dad and Sylvia afterward that I was going to the diner and that someone else would drive me home. And then six of us squeezed into a booth and ordered a communal platter of waffles, sausage, and eggs.

A tall guy in a Redskins cap held up a bite of scrambled egg and studied it. "The hen who laid the egg was a miracle," he said in mock reverence.

It didn't lessen the miraculous feeling that just being alive at all was so hugely special.

I was *so* not caught up with homework. Printouts of college campuses, along with notes and phone numbers, were in a heap on one side of my desk. I had to spend the rest of Sunday afternoon and most of the evening on a physics assignment I didn't understand and an essay for English on the twentieth-century novel. Sylvia said they were going to have a tray supper in the family room watching *60 Minutes*—did I want to eat with them? I opted for dinner in my room, knowing I couldn't afford the distraction. I promised myself that I could call Patrick at ten, but only if I finished both assignments.

It was about nine when my cell phone rang, and I reached for it eagerly.

There was nothing in my promise that said I couldn't talk with Patrick if he called first. But it wasn't a number I recognized.

"Hello?" I said.

"Good evening," said a voice.

"Hello?" I said again, questioning.

"I am calling to speak with Alice," came the voice, and then I recognized Daniel Bul Dau. "Am I speaking with Alice?"

"Daniel! Hi!" I said. "How *are* you? It was great to see you at the Homecoming Dance."

"It was a good evening," he said, each word enunciated with perfection. "I am telling my brother about the game and the dance, and he is doing same thing at the George Washington."

"Excuse me?" I said.

"The university," he explained. "Geri is a student there at the George Washington's University. That is how we get to America with my mother. We are all of us refugees, but he is also a scholarship there. We are very, very lucky."

"Well, we're lucky to have you at our school," I told him. "And I'm really looking forward to the article you're going to write for *The Edge*. You have a lot to tell us."

"I will tell you whatever you want to know," said Daniel. "And I have something else to tell."

"What's that?"

"I am calling to take you big Snow Ball."

"What?"

"I am hearing about another dance, a Snow Ball dance. I am inviting you to be my guest."

The invitation, or the statement, seemed to hang in the air in front of me, the letters dancing up and down. Was he serious? Daniel had only been in this country a few months. He had only been in our school since September. He had learned to dance only the night before. But what other answer could there be?

"Sure," I said.

Was he ready for this? Was I?

5

The Meaning of Eight

I didn't call Patrick, I called Gwen.

"What am I going to *do*?" I said in a panic.

"What do you mean? You're going to the dance with him. We taught him to dance, remember?"

"But . . . what about all the other stuff? The tickets, the flowers, where we eat before the dance? He probably doesn't have a clue. He doesn't have a car. He doesn't drive. Gwen, he's a refugee! He doesn't have anything!"

Gwen sure put me down in a hurry. "Then I guess you should have said, 'No, Daniel. You're a refugee. You don't have anything.'"

I could feel the flush in my cheeks. Gwen had never said something like that to me before.

"You're not being fair," I snapped. "Who's going to clue him in about what he should wear and what's expected of him?"

She was more patient now, but I still wasn't home free. "Well, what *should* we expect of a refugee? Why can't he wear whatever he likes and celebrate his originality? Does he *have* to come in a black-and-white penguin suit? Does he have to have big bucks in his pockets? Is there a rule that says *you* couldn't drive to the dance?"

I don't know what it was—shame, perhaps—but she was so politically correct that I just said, "Thanks, Gwen," and hung up. I'd never done that before either. I sat on the edge of my bed, cell phone in my lap, hugging myself.

Just fifteen minutes ago I had been eating a bowl of chili, writing an essay for English, feeling like I had a grip on my life, and now I was going down a sinkhole.

The phone rang again. *Not Patrick! Please, not Patrick!* I picked it up. It was Gwen.

"Relax," she said. "You can double with Austin and me. We'll think of something."

The school was still in high spirits on Monday. Balloons confiscated from the dance were tied to locker doors, and streamers flew from car antennas in the parking lot. Kids were already talking about the next game and the next.

I was heading to the staff room after school to go over the layout of the paper when Daniel caught up with me, his smile taking up the whole of his face.

"I am pleased you will go to the Snow Ball with me," he said.

"Thanks for inviting me," I said. "I think it will be loads of fun."

"It will be a . . . a number one for me. A first," he said. "I asked my brother about it, but he doesn't know anything about snowballs."

"We'll work out the details later," I told him. "It's not until the first week of December, so we don't have to do anything right now."

"So many customs," Daniel said, walking along beside me. Then he stopped and pulled something out of his notebook, handing it to me, his smile a bit more bashful.

"I find this in my locker this morning. It is . . . drawn by the hand? I am thinking it is maybe from you? It means a girl says thank you?"

I studied the index card in my hand. There were no words, just a circle. And inside the circle, two figure eights, side by side.

"It's not from me," I said, puzzled. "I really don't know what it means. Maybe someone on the newspaper staff would know. Want me to take it and ask around?"

"Okay," said Daniel. And then, "Perhaps another girl is wanting me to take her to the dance?"

I had to laugh at his cocky self-assuredness. "Hey, Daniel, if you change your mind, go for it," I teased.

"No, I did not mean that! But I don't under-stand all your customs."

"I don't either," I said. "But when I find out about this one, I'll let you know."

In the newsroom everyone was gathered around Sam's photos from homecoming week-end, spread out on one of our long tables. We each had our own opinion about which six pho-tos we should use and whether to save some for the following issue.

"Wish we got one of the streakers," I said, grinning.

"So does the faculty," said Phil.

We decided on a shot of Pam and Gwen teach-ing Daniel to dance, for starters. And of course we had to use an image of the float carrying the homecoming king and queen. The one of the win-ning touchdown . . . a close-up of the crowd . . .

The roving reporters checked in with their quotes and left, and it was finally down to Phil, Tim, Sam, Miss Ames, and me to make the final decisions. When we'd about wrapped things up, I remembered the index card in my bag and pulled it out.

"Hey, Phil," I said. "Any idea what this is? Daniel Bul Dau found it in his locker this morn-ing. He asked what it meant. I haven't a clue."

Phil stared at it a minute, then at me. "You've never seen one of these before?"

"No. What is it? Please don't say it's porn."

"You might call it that," Phil murmured, and showed it to Tim. "The two eights are shorthand for the eighth letter of the alphabet, 'H.' Using two in a row stands for 'Heil Hitler.'"

"I don't believe this!" I gasped.

"It's a Nazi symbol. Believe it," said Phil.

We sat around the conference table looking at the two eights. Nobody wanted to touch it, like maybe it should be dusted for fingerprints or something.

"Nice welcome to our school, isn't it?" said Sam. "Hey, I'm Jewish. Where's mine? Who's next?"

Phil looked at Miss Ames. "Should I do an editorial on it?"

Miss Ames is a thin woman with an oval face and small features, straight brown shoulder-length hair. Now she studied the card with her hands locked beneath her chin, fingers covering her mouth. Finally she said, "I think that, for now, we should just sit on it. What white supremacy groups want more than anything else is public-ity. For us to come on full force, in full battle regalia, just because somebody drops this pitiful little card in a locker, would be giving them more attention than they deserve."

I wasn't sure about keeping it under our hat, though. I thought of something we'd discussed at church—that the greatest wrong is not that evil exists in the world, but that good people sit by and do nothing. Something like that. Weren't newspapers supposed to find out what was going on beneath the surface and inform the public?

"Maybe we do more harm just by opting out," I said. "Maybe there's more than one person behind this."

"There's that possibility too. I'll show the card to Mr. Beck. But my guess is that this is a single act by a coward and that no acknowledgment at all would be the best response."

"And if there *is* more than one person involved, maybe they'll do something else to get attention, and then it might be easier to flush them out," said Phil.

We mulled that over awhile.

"Except that things might already be going on that we don't know anything about," said Sam, absently turning his Coke can around and around on the table. "Isn't there a new club here—SSC—Student Safety Council, I think? What's that about? Maybe they've got wind of stuff like this on campus."

"We sent one of our freshman reporters to check out the new clubs, and he visited that one last week. Said it was a small group—five or six. Talked with somebody named Butler, who said they focus on the dangers of drugs and alcohol, dealing with thugs, things like that," Phil said. "But that could mean that one of them has been attacked or something."

"Curtis Butler. I met him," I told the others. "He attended our last GSA meeting, Phil. Remember? Do you think there are gay students being harassed who never report it?"

"*The Edge* serves as the eyes and ears of the school," Miss Ames said. "Let us know of anything you find out. In the meantime, I'll give this card to Mr. Beck."

I wondered if we were right in not responding to this. As far as we knew, Daniel—because of his . . . what? race? nationality?—was the only one to get this card. But what about the other African-American students in our school? What about Curtis, if he was gay, or Lori and Leslie? What about socially challenged students like Amy Sheldon?

Sometimes the most difficult assignment of all is waiting to see what happens.

I was hoping that Daniel wouldn't ask me again about the double eights, but he asked the very next day. He absurdly stuck to his hope that it was a note of some kind from a girl. No bashfulness there.

"I'm afraid it wasn't," I said, looking up at him. "I asked around at our staff meeting, and it seems it's a Nazi symbol—just some jerk showing off his prejudice." I'd already told Miss Ames that I would tell Daniel the truth. I saw the puzzlement on his face. "We don't know who it's from, Daniel—some cowardly person—but please don't take this too seriously. I think you know that most of the students are glad to have you here."

You never forget the way a smile disappears.

"They told us before we left Sudan . . . that there are those like that in America," he said dispiritedly.

"Yeah. Unfortunately. And not just in America, as you know. Miss Ames turned the card over to our principal. *We're* the ones in charge, though, not the person who drew that thing."

"That is good to remember," Daniel said. And his smile came back, not quite what it was before.

I helped Sylvia with dinner that night and told her about the double eights. She teaches in middle schools, and was pondering the way they might have handled it if the card had been deposited there.

"We probably wouldn't do anything either if it were a single incident—a note, a scribble. You want to pick your battles and not bring too much attention to something stupid," she said. "But it's a shame it happened to Daniel."

"This is going to be the busiest semester of

my life," I told her, letting out my breath. "You solve one problem and something else pops up. I wish we had a mid-semester vacation."

"Patrick coming home for Thanksgiving?"

"I'm not sure. His family's been spending a lot of time at his uncle's in Wisconsin, but I think he said he was coming home." I gave Sylvia a wistful smile. "Hope so, anyway."

Marilyn Rawley Roberts was wearing real maternity clothes now. For the first four months of her pregnancy, she'd gotten by with denim jumpers and big shirts. Now when I went to the Melody Inn on Saturdays, I found her in the "official uniform," as she calls it—stretch pants and smock tops. Customers smiled and asked the due date (the end of February) and whether it was a boy or girl (Marilyn and Jack wanted to be surprised).

"Wow, Marilyn!" I said that Saturday when we were rearranging the CDs on a new rack. "I feel like I've known you since . . ."

"Forever," she said. "Since I was Lester's supposedly number one girlfriend." She laughed when she said it, without a trace of resentment or regret, which meant we could discuss it.

"Unfortunately, that's what several girls thought, I guess," I said, accepting the handful of CDs she gave me and putting them in alphabetical order on the rack. "You always seemed like . . . like Nature Girl or something to me."

"*Nature* Girl?" Her eyes widened for a second, then crinkled in laughter.

"In fact," I went on, "your wedding was exactly as I'd imagined it would be—in a meadow with wildflowers. Except . . . you'd be barefoot and the groom would be Lester."

"Yeah, well, sometimes life knows what's best for us, and I can't imagine being married to anyone else but Jack. I love him to pieces. How is Les, by the way? Did he ever finish his thesis?"

"Almost done. He graduates in December."

"Wonderful! Then what?"

"I don't know. He has a full-time job in the personnel department at the U. Maybe he'll stay there awhile, which means I could see him every day if I'm accepted."

"You're applying to Maryland?"

"And a few others. They have a good program in counseling." When she didn't respond, I asked, "Where did you think I would go?"

"I hadn't thought much about it, Alice. It's so entirely your business."

"Well, if *you* were graduating from high school this spring, and if Jack weren't in the picture, where would *you* have liked to go?" I asked.

"If money wasn't a consideration, you mean? Oh . . . Berkeley . . . USC; University of Seattle, maybe. Love that campus. Or some little college up in Maine."

I felt a prick of anxiety and a weight that settled in. "You wouldn't want to be closer to home? Friends and family?"

"I'd expect to make new friends. But when I settled down, like I am now, I'd want to be near my folks if I could, especially if I was planning a family. But college is our chance to explore a little."

"I just think . . . I mean, with the economy the way it is . . . and we're not exactly rich . . ."

"The University of Maryland is an excellent school, Alice, and will save your dad a heap of money," Marilyn said quickly. "You always were a considerate person. You'll do fine."

Our new clerk came back from lunch just then. At first Dad had considered hiring two new people when David Reilly left, as Marilyn would be going on maternity leave in February. But with sales down and some of the stores around us closing, Dad settled for one more full-time employee. Kay Yen was a college student, as David had been. She'd earned her bachelor's degree and wanted to take a year or two off and work to save some money before she started graduate school.

She and Marilyn got along famously from the start. They were both on the short side, and both had brown eyes. Marilyn had shoulder-length brown hair, however, while Kay's was short and black, turned under at the edges. Marilyn wore dangly gypsy-type earrings, while Kay wore tiny pearls in her earlobes. But when you heard them laughing together in the next room, you couldn't tell them apart.

"What did you major in?" I asked Kay, my mind still on college.

"Chemistry," she said as she cut open the next box and began stacking CDs on the counter. "I have a minor in music and was trained as a singer, but I'm really not good enough to do concert work, and I'm not sure I'd be happy teaching. So I guess I'll go into chemistry, my second love."

"You sound like the guy you replaced," I said. "He couldn't decide between marrying or entering the priesthood. He chose the priesthood."

"Well, I'm sort of letting my profession find me," said Kay. "My parents want me to marry and give them a grandchild. It's hard to think about having a child when you feel so much like one yourself."

That sure resonated with me. Maybe it's normal to feel so unsettled. Maybe there are more Lesters and Davids and Kays than I'd thought, and it's the unusual person who knows from day one just what she wants to do and where to go to school. "Brothers and sisters?" I asked Kay.

"I'm an only child. The one-child policy in China, you know," she said.

I thought about the card Daniel had found in his locker. "Do you feel welcome in America?" I asked her.

"Of course!" Kay replied. "I've lived in this country since I was six. But then, we've always lived in college towns. You can get complacent in a college atmosphere and feel that everyone in America accepts you. And that's not always the case."

6

Road to Chapel Hill

The Gay/Straight Alliance was celebrating National Coming Out Day on October 11, a day set aside to encourage gay, lesbian, bisexual, and transgender people to be themselves, to support them if they decide to "come out" to their friends and families. Just as *quarterback* defines only one part of who a student might be, Mr. Morrison likes to say, so does *gay* or *straight* represent only a part. "We are the sum of all our parts," we say at our meetings.

Some people call it International Awareness Day, so we had posters using both names. The GSA had been working on a huge paper rainbow, and some of us got to school early that Monday morning to attach it to the arch just inside the main entrance. We had rainbow armbands available on a little table outside the auditorium for students to wear to show support for everyone's sexual orientation.

Daniel Bul Dau was clearly shocked when he saw two guys greet each other at the table with a kiss.

"In my country," he told us, "we would be put to death. There is no such homosexuality in Sudan."

"Really?" asked Phil. "Then who do they put to death?"

Daniel seemed confused. "If there is homosexuality, I have never heard one speak of it. And not with rainbows. But I will ask my brother about it."

A lot of kids paused to look the table over and pick up a brochure. Curtis Butler was one of them. Others stopped to ask questions, and a few accepted an armband.

Gwen and Pam, Liz and I sat out under a tree at lunchtime along with Lori and Leslie. Leslie was telling how she came out to her mom a couple of years before, when she and Lori started hanging out a lot.

"Mom was trying to get me interested in a guy down the street—his mom was in her book club—and I decided I just had to tell her or else she'd go on pressuring me all through high school," she said.

Lori listened sympathetically, though she must have heard this story a dozen times.

"Finally, when I'd run out of excuses," Leslie

continued, "I said, 'Mom, I really don't want to go out with guys. I'm a lesbian.'"

"My mom would freak out," Pamela interrupted. "She really would. To her, that would be worse than . . . worse than me getting pregnant. And she'd blame herself."

"Well, it was a relief, mostly," Leslie said. "I never worried she'd kick me out or anything. I guess I wasn't sure *how* she'd handle the news. She just stared at me for a minute; then she laughed and said, 'You are *not*! Don't be ridiculous.' It took me an hour or more to convince her. She just sat there shaking her head. Sometimes I think that she still doesn't believe it and that if I could ever just meet the right guy . . ."

"That's the way it was with my parents," said Lori. "It wasn't till I reached way back and told them how I'd felt when I was five and six that they began to understand. How I'd always hated dresses, loved my truck collection, cried when I got a Barbie doll instead of a G.I. Joe. They began to see that this wasn't just a temporary phase because some guy rejected me or something. Our parents can't seem to imagine *us* ever rejecting *guys*."

We smiled at the thought—Lori, tall and brunette; Leslie, a natural blonde, shorter, sturdy . . . both of them pretty.

Liz picked up her egg salad sandwich. "What

I *can* imagine," she said, "is feeling entirely out of step with everyone else—feeling that what I wanted was natural to me but seemed unnatural to other people. And what *they* wanted for *me* seemed disgusting."

"And the more they try to 'fix it,' the more unnatural it feels," said Leslie.

"Daniel told me that homosexuals in his country would be killed for it," I said.

"Well, people in this country have been killed for it too," said Gwen.

That afternoon, as the buses were pulling up at the main entrance, I saw a small crowd gathering inside.

"What's going on?" I asked a girl who was walking away, shaking her head.

"Go look," she said.

I did. The large paper rainbow we had constructed was still hanging overhead, but there was a little pile of rainbow armbands on the floor beneath it, bent and crumpled, like trash. And on top of the little heap, a hand-lettered sign in Magic Marker: FAG DROPPINGS.

The administration had debated how they should handle this, Miss Ames told the newspaper staff. There were pros and cons about giving these incidents any publicity—treating them as anything more than scribbles on a restroom wall. One of the GSA guys had cleaned up the pile of armbands quickly before too many kids had even seen it. We'd heard no rumors, picked up no gossip, and Miss Ames said that the next step might be to send out our roving reporters on an investigative mission, armed with the right question. Perhaps that would give us some clues.

But choosing the right question itself caused a debate among the staff. We first proposed *What do you fear most about your safety here at school?* but decided that was too suggestive. The question *Is there anyone or any group here at school that makes you feel intimidated?* sounded as though we were pointing the finger at someone. We finally decided on *What, if anything, makes you fear for your safety here at school?*

The B-team reporters promised to go to work on it and would turn in some replies by the following Monday.

With the teachers' in-service training day coming up, and therefore our three-day weekend, I called Les that night and left a message on his cell phone.

"Remember, Les? This is the weekend you promised! UNC on Friday, William and Mary on Saturday, George Mason on Sunday. And you can be home in time to watch the Redskins play at four. I already checked their schedule. How early do you want to come on Friday? Call me."

Then I sat down at my computer, went to Yahoo for directions, and printed out a map of the whole trip—drive south to Chapel Hill, northeast to Williamsburg, then back up to Fairfax before heading home. The map planner gave me the routes, the travel times, and local attractions. I checked my notes. I was pretty sure I had a dorm room assignment for Friday night—I was supposed to call someone at Welch Hall; I was waiting for a callback about Saturday. I'd received a brochure from George Mason, a packet from Maryland, another from Chapel Hill. . . .

The phone rang Wednesday night. "*This* weekend?" Les bellowed.

"Yes!" I said. "Lester, I already *told* you! You *promised*!"

A huge sigh followed by silence.

"It's my only three-day weekend this fall! I've got to see some colleges before I apply, and you have to admit you owe me one, because—"

"Okay, okay, let me think, will you? It's . . . what? Three hundred miles to Chapel Hill?"

"Two hundred ninety-three."

"Al, have you got *everything* planned?"

"Yes. I told you! I've got the maps and the mileage and—"

"Where am I staying?"

"What do you mean?"

"You're staying overnight on campus, right? Where am I staying? Have you checked out motels?"

Omigod! Lester! "Right. Um . . . I've got the numbers right here. I'll have it all down for you in black and white."

"When's your first appointment on Friday?"

"Two o'clock," I said.

"We need to allow five hours, minimum. Six, if we stop to eat."

"I'll call you about the details," I said. "Dad said he'll pay all expenses."

"Okay. I'll fill my tank."

"Thanks, Les!" I said cheerfully. "We'll have a ball!"

"Right," said Les.

A few minutes after I'd talked with Lester, Patrick called.

"How are things?" he asked.

"Crazy," I told him. "We're seeing three schools this weekend. Lester's driving me to UNC, William and Mary, and George Mason."

"All in one weekend?" he asked.

I sucked in my breath and let it out again as I plopped down on the edge of my bed. "Yes, Patrick. Three schools in three days. Is that so unusual?"

This time I could hear the amusement in his

voice. "What are you going to do? Sample the food in the dining hall, check out the student union, and move on?"

"I'm going to get a feel for each place. I think I can at least rule some of them out after I've been there. This doesn't mean I can't visit one again if I really like it."

"How did you rope Les into this?" he wanted to know.

"Brownie points," I said. "He owes me big-time for a lot of things."

"Wow! You're keeping score. So what else is happening?"

"Well . . ." I smoothed out my bedspread with one hand. "I guess I'm going to the Snow Ball."

"Oh!" Now I really had his attention. "Who's the lucky guy?"

"Daniel Bul Dau."

"Who? Do I know him?"

"No. He's from Sudan."

"So . . . what's he like?"

"Tall, dark, and handsome," I teased. "Even taller than you are."

"Should I be jealous?"

"Wouldn't hurt," I said. "Actually, he's very nice. Polite."

"You invited him?"

"No. He invited me. And I didn't know what to say, Patrick. Gwen got on my case because I wondered if he was up to it, but he doesn't really know much about our culture. I think he's a little overconfident because we taught him a few steps at the Homecoming Dance."

"Well, someone will clue him in," said Patrick. "Lucky Daniel."

"What have *you* been doing?" I asked.

"Catching up on Bollywood movies," he said. "I've missed most of them, but we're having an Indian film festival, so I walk over to Ida Noyes when I can."

I took a chance. "By yourself?"

"And whoever else wants to go. You met John and Adam and Fran, I think."

"Yes . . ."

"They go sometimes. I even sat beside one of my professors last week. He was there with his girlfriend."

"You're getting up in the world, Patrick," I joked.

"Yeah, before you know it, I'll have a graduate assistantship, teaching nerds like me." We laughed, but he didn't exactly answer what I wanted to know.

We talked for another twenty minutes, and then I said, "You're coming home for Thanksgiving, aren't you?"

"Well, actually . . ."

I couldn't breathe.

"My folks want to have Thanksgiving at my uncle's house in Wisconsin."

"Oh, Patrick! I haven't seen you since—"

"I know. Mark's funeral. I'm disappointed too."

"They were just *in* Wisconsin! I mean—" I stopped. What right did I have to decide where Mr. and Mrs. Long should spend the holiday?

"But I'll definitely be home for Christmas," Patrick said.

"That's a long way off."

"Two months, is all."

"Ten weeks."

"You miss me?"

"More than you can imagine. I thought of you all during the homecoming parade. . . ."

By the time we'd finished talking it was nine thirty and I went back to the website I'd bookmarked to confirm that I was signed up for the Friday tour at two. Then I found the website for William and Mary and clicked on TOURS to sign up for Saturday. *Two p.m. filled*, it read. Next available tour: three weeks.

By Thursday it seemed as though every teacher had assigned a little more homework, just to fill up our three-day weekend. One teacher did say that those who were planning to visit colleges over the weekend would have three extra days to get their assignments in.

I hadn't even thought about what I'd be taking with me to visit schools. Hadn't checked to see if I had any clean pajamas. Hadn't made motel reservations yet for Les. For a girl who might be leaving home in less than a year, I was pitifully unprepared. Somehow I'd thought that signing up for a tour was no big deal. Colleges were always happy to show students around, right? How could William and Mary be filled? I called George Mason directly and asked about tours, but they didn't have a tour that Sunday.

The lonesome, homesick, panicky feeling returned as I pulled a duffel bag out from under my bed and opened it, trying to organize my thoughts: jeans, top, T-shirts, sweater, sneakers, tampons, makeup kit. . . .

Next I looked up hotel chains in the Yellow Pages, called some toll-free numbers and asked if they had any locations near the UNC campus. The closest I could find was a motel called Sleepy Inn, and I made a reservation for Les for Friday night. Then I did the same thing for Williamsburg and got a Ramada.

Les called around seven. "You find a place for me in Chapel Hill?"

"Yep, and my tour's at two," I said.

"I think we should leave at eight, then. Make it seven thirty if you want to stop and eat somewhere."

"I'll bring sandwiches," I said.

He must have sensed the tension in my voice. "And, Al," he said, "hang loose."

Dad and Sylvia were falsely impressed with my arrangements. Dad was absolutely gleeful, I think, that he didn't have to drive. "Any expenses within reason," he said, handing me his credit card.

"Hope all goes well!" said Sylvia.

My hair was filthy, so I set my alarm for six thirty, and hoped to be asleep by eleven. But I realized I still hadn't received a callback about my request for a place to sleep at William and Mary. I tried the number I'd called before, but no one answered. Then I called the number I had for Welch Hall, to confirm my room at Chapel Hill, and got voice mail. I left a message that I was arriving Friday and would drop off my bag there.

By the time I did get to bed, I was wakeful and didn't drift off till after midnight. I dreamed I was in a room that kept getting smaller, and I couldn't tell if the walls were moving closer together or the ceiling was coming down or what. When the alarm went off, I sprang out of bed as though it were on fire, glad to be out of the dream, I guess.

Later, when I opened the fridge, I found a

lunch Sylvia had already packed for us, but this just proved how dependent I'd become, always having someone there to look out for me, remind me, encourage me, pick up the tab. I thought about Patrick at the University of Chicago, getting right to work, fitting in, doing assignments, learning his way around. . . .

I was sitting on the steps when Les pulled up a couple minutes past eight, and I could tell he saw this as a mission of mercy, not a pleasure trip.

"Good morning!" I chirped as I got in, dropping my bag in back.

"Morning," he said. He reached for his Starbucks cup and took a long drink.

We were two blocks away when I realized I'd left my folder with all the necessary addresses and brochures in it, and we had to go back. While I was in the house, I remembered I'd also left the lunch Sylvia had prepared, so I got that, too.

"Better now than later," I said as I climbed back in the car, and at last we were headed for the beltway.

I took out my map and directions and began to read aloud: "Take ramp onto I-495 West toward Beltway/Northern Virginia. Go 6.7 miles. Continue on I-495 South for 17.5 miles."

"What's the exit we're looking for?" asked Les.

"Uh, 57A/Richmond," I told him.

He took out one CD and put in another, lifted the Starbucks cup again, then rested his arm on the open window.

It was a beautiful October morning, and it was sort of exciting going somewhere with Lester, our bags in the backseat. I rolled down my window too and pretended we were in a convertible. A beautiful girl on her way to college. I smiled at a couple of guys who passed us in a truck, and they waved.

Les gave me a look. "Watch it," he said, and grinned.

There's not a lot to see from a beltway except cars, and even less after the exit. But I-95 South was worst of all, and we had to go 118 miles on it.

We stopped for a bathroom break, but Les wanted to eat as he drove to make sure I made my two o'clock campus tour.

"You're not going with me, are you?" I asked.

"No. I'm going to drop you off and pick you up in the morning. You have the address of my hotel?"

"Yes. It's called Sleepy Inn. And I'll give you Dad's credit card too. Boy, this is the life, isn't it, Les?" My hair was blowing around my face, and the warm breeze rustled the map in my hands.

"Pretty sweet," he said.

I'd noticed Les had brought some books and papers along with him and would probably be working on his thesis while I was visiting schools.

I thought about how many years he'd been in school and how he was finally almost finished. I tried to imagine Christmas and a college graduation both in the same month.

"Sometimes I wish I could just press a button and be through school and starting my real life," I told him.

"This *is* your real life, Al," he said. "Don't start living in the future. That's like gulping down a piece of fudge cake and then asking yourself, 'Where'd it go?' You're missing the moment."

"Ah! The philosopher is back," I said. "I know how to enjoy a moment, Les. I'm enjoying this, aren't I?"

"You'd better."

"Frankly," I told him, "I don't think about the future enough. Sometimes I can't even see what's coming right at me, and I get blindsided."

"Yeah? Anything in particular?"

"Our student from Sudan asked me to the Snow Ball, and it caught me off guard. I said yes."

"And?"

"I don't know what to expect."

"Well, neither does he. Obviously, though, he feels comfortable with you."

I sighed and rolled up my window halfway because my hair kept blowing in my mouth when I tried to talk.

Les glanced over at me. "How does Patrick

feel about you going with someone else?"

"I *hope* he's a little bit jealous, but he says he's comfortable with it. *Too* comfortable, maybe."

"Well . . ." Les drove for a while without speaking. Then he said, "He's hundreds of miles away, Al. He's there, you're here, life goes on. But nobody's written the last chapter."

"Meaning?"

"Just that what happens today or next week or next year isn't necessarily the way things are always going to be. As soon as you settle into a routine, life throws you a curveball. Sometimes you hit it, sometimes you don't."

"It sure threw a curveball when Mark died."

"Yeah. It sure did." He was quiet for a moment. "Getting back to Patrick, though . . ."

"He wants me to live it up my senior year, even though he's not here to share it with me."

"Smart boy."

"Which means that he plans to live it up his first year of college even though I'm not there to share it with *him*."

"Ditto."

"Which means that's why he doesn't mind that I'm going to the Snow Ball with somebody else, because that means that the equal opportunity rule is alive and well in Chicago." I turned to Lester. "You're not even thinking of marriage yet, are you?"

"Not really. Are *you*?"

"Of course not. But I'm curious: How many women do you think you will have dated before you find the right one? I mean, honestly, Les, not to get personal or anything, but how many girls have you been out with in your whole life up until now?"

"To the nearest hundred?"

"Seriously! There was Claire last year, Tracy, Lauren, Eva, Joy, Crystal, Marilyn . . . Any others?"

"Lord, yes. Gloria, Mickey, Maxie, Amy, Lisa, Josephine, Caroline . . ."

"Omigod, Les, did that say Exit 51/Durham/Atlanta? That's the one we were supposed to take!"

"Al, you're supposed to be navigating!"

"Turn around! Turn around!" I cried.

"Are you insane? This is a freeway. We have to go to the next exit."

Les was cussing, I was hyperventilating, and then we saw we hadn't missed it after all:

EXIT 51/DURHAM/ATLANTA, NEXT RIGHT.

Saved. Now all I had to do was pretend I knew what I was doing when we got to Chapel Hill.

7

Call Girl

Lester stopped in the driveway of an official-looking building. It was already past two, but I told Les I'd catch up with the tour.

"This where it starts?" he asked.

I was digging through my folder of papers and couldn't find where I'd written the starting place for the Chapel Hill tour. "I think so," I said. And then, when Les frowned, I leaned forward and took a quick look at the name of the building.

"Yep! This is it!" I said, and reached in back for my bag.

"What residence hall are you staying in?" he asked.

"Welch," I said.

"Okay. We've got a four-hour drive to Williamsburg, so we need to leave here at eight tomorrow morning. Nine at the latest. You okay with that?"

"Let's make it eight thirty. I'll be waiting right here on the steps," I answered, leaning forward again to memorize the name of the building, Jackson Hall. I pulled my bag out after me. "Thanks loads, Lester!"

"Have fun! Ask questions! Check out everything!" he said.

"What are *you* going to be doing?" I asked.

"Walk a little. Eat a bite. I brought some work with me," he said, nodding toward his old briefcase in back, stuffed with his thesis.

The car pulled away, and I took a few steps forward to show I was at least in motion, duffel bag over my shoulder, a folder of papers in my hand. But my inability to find the notes I'd made on Chapel Hill made my mouth dry. I had the catalog of undergraduate studies, the admission form, tuition chart. . . . Even if I *had* known where the tour was starting out, I would have missed the first fifteen minutes by now.

I was walking over to the steps to sit down and look for my campus map when I saw a small group of people walking by. There were fifteen or so, both teens and adults, following a female guide who was walking backward and talking to them. The campus tour!

I waited for them to pass, and then slowly, nonchalantly, I sauntered after them, a short distance behind. I couldn't hear everything the guide was saying, but I could at least see whatever she was pointing out.

If I were in a movie playing the part of a spy, everybody in the audience would have guessed it was me. *Which person in this picture does not belong?* The girl with the duffel bag, pretending to study the trees.

"Perhaps some of you aren't aware of our rich two-hundred-year history," the cheerful guide was saying as I transferred the bag to my other shoulder. "We'll talk about that next. . . ."

There were times I got a little too close to the group and some of them looked at me warily, as though I might have a bomb in my bag. And once, when I was standing on tiptoe, trying to see what the guide was pointing out, she stopped a moment and said, "Excuse me, can I help you?"

I had no name tag like the others. I had not started out with the group. I wasn't even sure this was the right tour. I murmured that I was looking for the admissions office. Then everyone turned and stared at me as the guide replied, "Well . . . that's where the tour started: Jackson Hall."

My face aflame, I walked into the first building I came to and found a café. I ordered an iced tea and a doughnut and collapsed on a chair.

Why hadn't I come right out and said who I was and how I was late for a tour, and whoever they were, did they mind if I tagged along? Why hadn't I at least asked the guide to direct me to Welch Hall? If I couldn't speak up about something as minor as this, did I belong in college at all? Everyone else on campus seemed to know what they were doing and where they were going. Everyone else had a plan.

By the time I'd finished the doughnut, though, I was feeling a little better. I decided I'd find the residence hall first, drop my bag, and explore the campus on my own.

The campus was huge—*huge*—but I had a map, and I spread it out on the table. Then, with my duffel bag hoisted over my shoulder once more, I set out to find Welch, the University Plaza (aka "the Brickyard"), the Memorial Bell Tower, the Free Expression Tunnel underneath the railroad tracks, where anyone could paint graffiti. . . . There was a lot to see.

I tramped all around, but not only could I not find any of these places, I couldn't even find the right streets. I asked a student where I'd find the University Plaza, and he said he didn't know.

Even though I kept transferring my bag from one shoulder to the other, both shoulders were sore. Finally I sat down on a bench and took out my cell phone. I looked through my notes again and this time found the number for Welch Hall, punched in the number, and waited. Someone answered—a student, probably.

"Hi, I'm Alice McKinley, here for a student visit, and I can't find Welch Hall," I said.

"It's a huge campus, I know," the girl said comfortingly. "Can you tell me where you are now? Maybe I can direct you."

I looked around. "I'm sitting on a bench facing the Memorial Building."

"The Memorial Tower?"

"I . . . guess so. I don't see a tower."

"Are you anywhere near the Brickyard? I could probably direct you from there," she said.

"I can't find that, either. I've even picked up a copy of the *Daily Tar Heel*, but—"

"*The Tar Heel?*" came the voice. "Are you sure you're at North Carolina State?"

I felt as though I were on an elevator and was plummeting toward the basement. "I'm right here at Chapel Hill," I told her.

"We're in *Raleigh*," the girl said. "Who were you supposed to see at Welch Hall?"

It was like one of those dreams where you suddenly discover it's the day of your midterm exam and you haven't studied for it. Not only haven't you studied, but you haven't opened the book. Not only have you not opened the book, you haven't attended class since school started, and you don't even know where the class is.

"My God!" I gasped. I wondered if I was going to pass out. I felt light-headed and dizzy. "I'm just checking out colleges. I thought someone said I could stay there tonight."

"Wow," the girl said. "Even if you wanted Raleigh, Welch doesn't have any room for visitors. We're full up."

"I—I wanted Chapel Hill. But I—I must have brought the wrong map. S-Sorry to have bothered you," I said quickly, and hung up.

I sat there breathing in and out, in and out, one hand on my chest. Maybe I was having a heart attack. Finally, when the throbbing noise in my ears began to fade, I decided that the only thing left to do was find my way back to Jackson Hall and throw myself on the mercy of the admissions staff. But I was exhausted and stopped at the student union for the special of the day, glad to drop my bag at a table by the window.

I got my chicken à la king on toast and began shuffling through my papers again in a state of disbelief. Somehow I had printed out information on both North Carolina State at Raleigh and the University of North Carolina at Chapel Hill, and most of what I'd brought along, including the campus map, was for North Carolina State.

But they're both in North Carolina, right? I asked myself. Both schools had the words *North* and *Carolina* in them. I quickly thumbed through every paper I had and found only a page or two about Chapel Hill. I yanked the duffel bag from the floor to my lap and thrust the papers back inside.

"You hitchhiking cross-country?" a guy asked.

He'd taken the empty seat across from me, and his feet had collided with mine. I took it as a joke and laughed a little. "No, I'm checking out colleges this weekend and have to carry this with me until I find a place to crash," I said.

He took an analytical approach: "You could always try the gym," he said. "We heard of a guy who hung out there for three days before maintenance threw him out. Used the showers, a locker—slept on an exercise mat. Probably find one of those in the women's locker room." He was serious!

"Thanks," I said. "I'll look into it."

"I hiked the Appalachian Trail one summer," he said, and pushed his glasses back up the bridge of his nose. The stems were too long, though, because the glasses slid right down again. "Not all of it. Got through South Carolina and part of Georgia, and then I got dysentery and had to quit."

"Bummer," I said, and got up to return my tray.

I went straight back to Jackson Hall, but the admissions office was closed.

What was this, a death wish? I grabbed my cell phone again and called the number I had for William and Mary, where I had originally left a message about needing a place to stay. All I got was the same automated voice asking me to leave a message. I ended the call and sat watching students walking by in little groups of three or four. Classes were over for the week, and people were calling out to each other, making plans for some Friday-night fun.

Okay, I told myself. *If all that is left for me is a Friday night at Chapel Hill, I'll at least sample that.*

There was a movie that evening on campus. I'd read the postings on a bulletin board. It was an Italian film revival, and one of Fellini's films was playing. You could get in for a dollar, so I went. I sat in the middle of a row so people could exit on either side of me, and used the duffel bag as a footrest.

There were no subtitles, though; the whole film was spoken in Italian, and I realized after a while that most of the audience understood it. This might even have been an assignment, because sometimes somebody translated a line aloud. I fell asleep toward the end, and when I woke, the lights had come on and people were leaving. I dragged my duffel bag into a restroom and used the toilet, then hauled it again to my shoulder and went outside.

It was raining—a light but steady rain that was more than a passing shower, I could tell. The sidewalk was slick with pine needles, and I hadn't brought an umbrella.

I followed a group of students to a chili dog shop, but all the tables were full, so I ate mine standing at a little counter by the window, one foot on my bag, listening to a group of guys argue about the Tar Heels' chances against the Terrapins.

The chili dog didn't agree with me and I needed a restroom again, so I found one of the libraries and used theirs. When I came back out and walked by the large reading room, it looked as though some students came to study all night. Several had stacks of books and papers scattered around them on the table, and I didn't see any sign indicating library hours. Hadn't I heard Les talk sometimes of "pulling an all-nighter" at the library?

I went in, dropped my duffel bag on a chair, got out my pen and notebook, laid my head on my arms, and drifted off.

I must have been more tired than I thought, because I woke finally to a series of thumps against my chair. I opened my eyes and had to lift my head slowly because there was a crick in my neck.

The custodian had bumped the legs of my chair with his vacuum and apologized in Spanish. Only a couple of students were still in the library, and the clerk at the desk was looking at me without smiling. I sat up and rubbed my neck. The clerk came over.

"Excuse me," he said. "May I see your ID card?"

"Uh . . . I'm just visiting the campus," I said.

"The library's for university students and faculty only," he told me, and glanced down at my duffel bag. "Sorry."

"That's okay. I didn't mean to fall asleep." My mouth felt crummy. "Is there any place on campus I could stay overnight?"

He shook his head and glanced up at the wall clock. Two minutes past eleven. "Have you tried the YMCA?" he said.

I went back outside. It was still raining. Still steady. I wondered whether the gym was open and couldn't remember where I'd passed it on campus. I really needed a shower. Really needed to wash my feet. I stuffed my purse and my cell phone into the duffel bag to keep them dry and started to walk.

There were lights on in a hamburger shop and a bookstore, but I knew they'd be closing soon. The streetlights would be on all night, but they didn't do me much good. Beyond the streetlights, I could see the outline of a department store and office buildings against the night sky. And beyond them, the glow of a neon sign, a huge eye—now open, now closed—and the words SLEEPY INN: VACANCY.

I shifted my duffel bag, turned up the collar

of my jacket, and with my sneakers sloshing and squeaking through the puddles, I headed up the street.

A light in still another store went out, then another across the street. I knew I shouldn't be out alone at this hour in a neighborhood I didn't know— even a university neighborhood—and I kept my eyes on the Sleepy Inn sign in the distance.

The rain was pelting down even harder as I approached the motel, and I hurried my steps as I went up the sidewalk. The small lobby was empty, and when I pulled on the door handle, I found that the door was locked. I couldn't believe this. The lights were on, but no one was at the desk.

Then a man came in from a back room and spread a newspaper out on the desk. I rattled the door handle. He looked up, pressed a buzzer, and the door unlocked. I went inside, my wet sneakers leaving footprints on the tile.

"Help you?" the clerk asked in monotone. He had a long, thin face with deep creases on either side of his mouth. He made no effort to hide the newspaper, probably sensing I wasn't a serious customer.

"Yes. My brother's staying here, and I wondered if you could tell me his room number," I said, realizing that my jacket was dripping water too.

The man studied me. My wet hair. My duffel bag.

"Your brother?" he asked, cocking his head to one side, a trace of sarcasm in his voice.

"Yes. Lester McKinley. He checked in this afternoon."

I saw the outline of the man's tongue in his cheek. He slowly put the newspaper aside and checked his computer. I could see only half the screen. Then he looked at me again. "You live around here?"

"No. I'm . . . sort of checking out the university," I told him.

"Your name?"

"Alice. He *knows* me!" I said impatiently.

"I'll phone his room and tell him you're here," he said.

The last thing Les needed to hear was that his dripping, drippy sister was standing in the lobby soaking wet, with no place to go. I had to handle this myself.

"Can't you just tell me his room number?" I begged.

"No. Sorry." He pressed a three-digit number, listened for a moment. "Busy," he said, and hung up.

"Well, I'll wait," I said, and tried to shake some water out of my hair. The clerk frowned as some of it hit his desk. "Sorry," I said quickly, and patiently stood aside. The clerk went back to reading his newspaper.

A minute went by. Two. Three. Les could be on the phone with a girlfriend, if he had a girlfriend. Or maybe he'd just taken the phone off the hook. After another minute of waiting, I said, "Could you try again, please?"

The look again. The tongue in the cheek. But this time I studied closely as he pressed the three-digit number: 2 . . . 1 . . . 7. I'd bet that was his room number.

"Busy," the man said again, and hung up.

"I guess I'll just have to wait," I said.

I dragged my wet bag over to the vinyl couch and sat down. The clerk folded up one section of the paper and opened another. Two more minutes went by. Three.

I knew the desk clerk wouldn't try the phone again until I begged. He enjoyed making me plead. I thought of digging out my cell phone and calling Les on that, but I had a better idea.

"Excuse me, could I use the restroom?" I asked. And when he looked up without answering, I said, "It's urgent."

He gave me a disgusted look, then nodded toward a doorway behind him. "Back there," he said, and added, "Keep it neat."

I walked to one side of his desk and through the doorway with my bag. It led to a side hall.

There was a restroom marked EMPLOYEES ONLY on the left and, just down the hall, an elevator.

It took only a second to decide. I opened the door of the restroom and let it close again without going inside. Then, when the clerk turned a page of his paper and leaned over it again, I edged my way down the hall to the elevator. I pressed the button and the door slid open. I got on and pressed 2.

8

Night in Chapel Hill

Oh, man! I wondered how long it would take Mr. Sarcastic down at the desk to go to the door of the bathroom to check if I was still in there. How long before he simply barged in? Would he figure out what I'd done? Probably.

The elevator door didn't open immediately when it reached the second floor. I panicked at the thought of the elevator getting stuck, how I'd have to push the alarm button and scream. And how the clerk, guessing it was me, would take his time calling 911.

Then the elevator door groaned and slowly slid open. I sprang out, checked the numbers on the doors, and made a left to room 217.

There was no sound from inside. I knocked lightly.

Still no sound. What if the room number wasn't the same as the phone number? What if I woke up a stranger? I knocked again, a little more desperately, and heard a toilet flush. Then the door opened, and there stood Les in his boxer shorts and a tee.

"Al! What the heck?" he said.

I darted inside and closed the door after me. One of the beds was strewn with books and papers, pillows piled up against the headboard. Lester's cell phone was charging on the second bed.

"What *happened*?" Les asked, still standing by the door as though he expected me to leave momentarily.

"It was getting late, and I didn't know the neighborhood," I told him. "Please let me stay, Les. I screwed up."

"What do you mean? They couldn't find a place for you to sleep?"

I took off my wet jacket and put it in his bathtub, then came out and slumped down in the one chair. "Well . . . yeah, that too," I said in a small voice. "But . . . I got the wrong school."

He stared at me. "You . . . *what*?"

I curled into a fetal position. "I got things mixed up and brought the map and notes for Raleigh. North Carolina State."

Les just kept staring at me. "We're supposed to be at *Raleigh*?"

"No, we're supposed to be here, but . . . Oh, Les, I just really goofed up. I'd Googled a lot of schools and printed stuff out before I chose the ones I did, and I brought the wrong map along."

"But you said you had a room in a residence hall."

"It was in Raleigh, and I didn't know it. I *thought* I had a room, anyway, but when I called they said they were full, so even if we'd gone there . . ."

"*Damn*, Al! You didn't plan for Chapel Hill at all? We drove all the way down here just to hang out at the Sleepy Inn?"

"Don't yell at me, Les," I mewed. "I checked out the campus. The library. I ate somewhere on campus—I forget where."

"Great. You checked out the pizza." Les still hadn't moved. He stood with his arms crossed and glared at me.

"Les, I don't even know if I belong at Chapel Hill! If I could even get accepted. Everybody's weird and smart."

"How can you tell? You hardly even talked to anybody. Why did we come here at all?"

"Because I have to check out some schools. Dad would freak out if I didn't look at some. You know that." Then, trying to change the subject, I asked, "Who were you talking to on the room phone? The guy at the desk tried to call you a couple times, but the line was busy."

Les refused to be distracted. He leaned against the door, arms still folded, and said, "I was talking to Paul about a gift for George's wedding. As for you—"

At that moment someone knocked, and Les jumped. He turned around and peered through the peephole.

"Jeez!" he said. He gave me a look and opened the door.

A man stood there in a security uniform. "Excuse me," he said. "This room registered to one person? You Lester McKinley?"

"That's right," said Les. "And my sister just arrived. Seems she's spending the night."

Yes! I silently cheered.

"Your registration lists only one occupant," the security guy said.

"That's what I thought at the time," Les said.

It wasn't fair to make Lester take the rap for me, and I knew it. "I was supposed to spend the night somewhere else, and it didn't work out," I told the man.

I could tell I was making things worse.

"Identification?" he asked.

I reached for my bag on the floor and rummaged around till I found my wallet. I showed the guard my driver's license.

"You need to go down to the registration desk and sign in," he said. And to Les, "There's an additional charge for her."

"Okay," said Les. "Let me put on some pants."

The security guard put one hand against the wall outside and waited, to show he meant business.

Les let the door close and yanked on a pair of jeans.

"Les, I'm so sorry!" I kept saying. "I really didn't mean to cause trouble."

Silently, he got his sneakers from under the bed and thrust his feet inside them.

"Let's go," he said finally. I followed him out the door and down the hall, the security guard at my heels.

At the desk the clerk glowered at me, then at Les. In slow motion he reached for his pen and asked for my driver's license. He copied everything down—ID number, age, weight, address. Then he turned to the computer and slowly entered all the stuff he'd written by hand.

Les got the picture pretty quick. "Anything else?" he asked. "You want her passport? Birth certificate? Vaccination records?"

Mr. Sarcastic didn't even answer. Just printed out a new page, shoved it toward Les, and said, "Sign."

The elevator didn't seem to be working. Les kept pressing the buttons, but the door wouldn't close. We could hear mechanical grinding and groaning. The door started to close, then slid open again.

"What *else* can go wrong?" Les muttered. "Let's take the stairs."

We didn't know where they were, however. Les turned left, so I followed. We were halfway down the hall when a man called out, "Where you folks going?" We turned to see the security guy, hands on hips.

"Elevator's broken. We're looking for the stairs," Les said.

"This end," the guard told us, turning to lead the way, but he stopped when he came to the elevator. He reached inside and pressed a button. The doors slid closed but opened again when he pressed the button on the outside. He cocked his head to show his impatience with us.

Les shrugged and we got on. He pressed 2. The door slid closed and the elevator moved. But when we got to the second floor, the door wouldn't open.

"Dammit!" Les exclaimed. He pressed OPEN. Nothing happened. He pressed 1. Nothing.

"*Blast* it!" Les cried, and pressed the alarm button. Somewhere a loud bell sounded. There was no phone or intercom that we could see.

I sat down in one corner. I'd worried about being stuck in the elevator by myself but hadn't figured it would happen to me and Les.

Les looked dumbfounded. "Can you *believe* this? Could anything top this?"

"Yes," I said. "One of us could need a bathroom."

I saw Lester's face crinkle into a smile, and then we were both laughing. Les leaned against the wall, and his arm hit the alarm button again. It rang a second time, and this really set us off.

Now the security guard was on our case for good. I guess he was standing outside the elevator on the second floor and could hear us laughing. He banged on the door.

"*Excuse* me!" he yelled. He said something about waiting for emergency maintenance and how if that didn't work, he'd call the fire department. And please don't ring the alarm again—he knew where we were.

Les sat down beside me, our feet straight out in front of us.

"This place is a dump, isn't it?" I said. "Sorry. The price was right. I was trying to save Dad some money. Probably bedbugs too."

"And no hot water after midnight," Les joked.

"Was there even soap in the bathroom? Or is that extra?" I said.

"After they rescue us, they'll add 'rescue' to the bill," said Les.

We laughed some more, then grew quiet, listening to the sounds of mechanical tinkering coming from the elevator shaft.

Les sighed. "Okay. Give it to me straight," he said. "You don't have a place to stay tomorrow in Williamsburg either, right?"

"Yeah, but I'll find one, I promise."

He covered his eyes. "I don't *believe* this. And if you don't find one?"

"Well . . ." I searched desperately for a silver lining. "Did we ever do Williamsburg, Les? I mean, did Dad ever bring us? Once we're there, with its history and all . . ."

Les stared at me incredulously. "You're serious?"

"I don't mean that we should see Williamsburg in place of William and Mary," I said hastily. "I could look around the college first, and then we could do the sights in the afternoon."

He was shaking his head. "You really think we're going to get up in the morning, drive two hundred miles, visit a whole campus—the buildings, the library, the residence halls—and do Williamsburg in the afternoon? Are you insane?"

I could feel my face heating up, and I swallowed. Les turned away and sighed again. He was disgusted with me, I knew.

At that moment the elevator jerked slightly and the door slid open.

We scrambled to our feet and bounded out the door before it could close again. When we got to our room, Les put up the DO NOT DISTURB sign so we wouldn't have to face the security guard again.

He looked tired, and he nodded toward the second bed. "We've got to get an early start, so why don't you turn in," he said, removing his cell phone and unplugging it.

I picked up my bag, dug around for my pajamas, and took them into the bathroom.

Les had good reason for being disgusted with me, I told myself, staring into the mirror. This whole trip was a waste of time, a waste of gas. He had carted all his thesis stuff along, trying to use his time efficiently, and I had really goofed up.

When I came out and crawled in bed, Les said, "Ready?" and turned out the lamp. The room was black except for some light from the parking lot that came through the venetian blinds.

"I'm not ready for college, Les," I said into the darkness, my voice shaky.

"I'm not buying," he answered.

"I'm just stating facts. I'm not even sure I want to go."

"Cut it out, Al."

"Really! I used to dream about Liz and Pam and Gwen and me all going to college together, sharing a dorm room. . . . It's not going to happen, Lester. We're all going off in different directions,

and Pamela may go to a design school or something. I'll have to make friends all over again with
a huge bunch of new people. . . ."

"Not all at once. You'll make friends just like
you made them in Silver Spring—one at a time."

"I just feel like . . . if I don't . . . if I can't make
friends . . . the right friends . . . if I screw that up,
I'll ruin my whole four years. I'll be homesick and
lonely and my grades will suck and—"

"What if I promise you that will never
happen?"

"You can't promise that, so I wouldn't believe
you."

"What if I promise that if you don't put a lid
on it, we're going straight home tomorrow, and
you can tell Dad the trip was a bust?"

"I believe you," I said, and after a long time I
fell asleep.

I felt better in the morning. My clothes were dry,
anyway, and Les let me have the bathroom first. I
got ready as fast as I could and decided I was going
to treat him to a good breakfast before we got on
our way. There was a new person at the desk.

"Room 217 checking out," Les said, handing
in his key card.

"I'll have your bill printed out in a moment,"
the young woman said cheerfully, checking the
computer.

"Is there a place nearby where we could get breakfast?" I asked.

"There certainly is," she answered, pulling a paper out of the printer and handing it to me. "There's a pancake house just around the corner, Mrs. McKinley. Enjoy!"

Lester's jaw dropped. He turned his head slowly and looked at me.

I howled when we got outside. "Must be my hair," I said. I'd piled it on top of my head that morning because I hadn't washed it, and I'd fixed it in place with a comb.

But Les was laughing too. "Get in," he said, slinging my bag in the back of his car and putting his briefcase beside it. "Man oh man, life with you is like living in a monkey house."

Over chocolate chip pancakes I asked him about George, the roommate who was getting married the following weekend. "Are you and Paul in the wedding?"

"Yeah, if it ever comes off. It was already delayed a month due to some scheduling problem," he said. "We're still trying to figure out what stuff is ours and what belongs to George."

I tried to imagine a bachelor pad with only two guys in it instead of three. "You've got three bedrooms," I said. "You going to get somebody else?"

"I don't know. We'll see what happens."

I thought about the four years of college ahead of me before I could graduate, and at least another year after that to get a master's before I could be a school counselor. Where would I live after I left home? By myself, or sharing an apartment?

"I'm glad you're going through all this first, so you can fill me in when it's my turn," I told him.

But Lester's disappointment in me really hurt. I knew myself that I'd prepared school assignments more carefully than I'd prepared for this trip, and I wanted Les to know that I was now serious. After our pancake breakfast and coffee, I paid the bill myself, and when we were on the road again, I paid attention:

"We're going to turn left on South Fordham Boulevard and go four miles," I instructed.

"I need route numbers," Les said.

"U.S. 15 North," I told him, map in my hand. "And then?"

"Go 7.2 miles, then merge onto I-85 North."

"Got it," he said.

It took three and a half hours, and we were hungry again when we got to Williamsburg. Because I didn't have a scheduled tour, we took time to get some hoagies at Ye Olde Sandwich Shoppe and enjoyed the costumed actors who passed by on the brick sidewalk occasionally, carrying on conversations with tourists as though it were back in the 1700s.

"All right," Les said when we'd finished eating. "You know where I'm staying, but let's not have a repeat of last night."

"We won't," I said. "First thing on my list is to find a place to crash."

"On *campus*," Les emphasized. "That's important."

I really did do better at William and Mary. Les let me off in front of the administration office, and I told the woman there that I didn't have a reservation for a tour but would like a map for a self-guided walk around campus. She was glad to help and told me to check one of the residence halls to see if any of the women would show me what the rooms were like. I heard her tell someone else that there was no place for visiting students to stay overnight, so I didn't ask, but I'd already made up my mind that I would pay for a motel myself if I couldn't sleep on campus, regardless of what Les had said.

I started off, duffel bag over one shoulder. *Welcome to William and Mary*, the brochure read, *one of America's oldest and best universities, which claims both Thomas Jefferson and Jon Stewart as alumni.* I "walked the brick pathways where Thomas Jefferson ran when he was late to class" and asked questions whenever I could, even when I knew the answer, just to sample the conversation.

The campus was smaller and more manageable than the one at Chapel Hill, more my style. *Next September this could be me*, I thought as I breezed along, my bag thumping against me. I could see myself as a student here on a fall morning, and when a guy smiled at me and said hi as he passed, I smiled back and thought, *Not bad!* I walked to the library, the sports center, the stadium—all the usual places, and was glad to put my duffel bag down at the bookstore and just browse and have an iced tea.

But I got really lucky in the caf, as they call their cafeteria, when a girl put her tray across from me on the table and, seeing the Moroccan chicken on my plate, said, "Oh, you love it too."

"It's great," I said.

"It's all I ever eat," she told me, and began shoveling food in her mouth. "I'm on a fifteen-minute break. Feed the dishwasher on Saturdays."

"Well, I'm visiting colleges this weekend," I told her. "My first time here."

"Yeah? Where you from?"

"Maryland. Silver Spring. I'm Alice."

"Judith," she said. She had short, dark, curly hair that seemed to bounce with every word. Dark, intense eyes, but friendly. "How do you like the school so far?"

"Nice," I said, "but I didn't make arrangements in advance, and my brother's sort of pissed. He drove me down and wants me to find a place to stay overnight on campus."

And just like that, Judith said, "You can stay with us. We're in a suite, and one of our roomies went home for the weekend. You could have her bed."

"Really?" I said. "How do you know she'd let me?"

"Because she loaned out my bed two weeks ago," Judith said. "Just don't leave makeup on her pillow. She hates that."

As she chewed the last bite of chicken, she scribbled the address of her residence hall on a paper napkin. "I'll meet you right here between five and five thirty," she said. "You can drop your bag off at the dorm."

"This is terrific," I said. "Thanks."

"Gotta run," she told me, and in one quick sweep, she slid her tray off the table and disappeared through the metal door leading to the kitchen.

9

Decisions

This was way too easy. I'd toured the campus myself—well, some of it, anyway—and I already had a place to sleep. I'd agreed to meet Les at nine o'clock in the morning right where he'd let me off, and he wasn't going to get a kid sister knocking on his motel door at midnight.

I spent the next couple of hours at the bookstore so that I didn't have to carry my bag and listened to the conversations going on around me to get a feel for the student life:

". . . I absolutely have to take another semester of Spanish or I can't graduate . . ."

". . . the best cookies! But if you want a fantastic fruit salad . . ."

". . . His face said it all. I mean, Rob's perfect for the part of Aaron, but I know Nick feels he should get the part . . ."

". . . the problem with the Drake equation is that he's only taken *this* galaxy into account, and when you consider the thousands of millions of galaxies . . ."

Judith got off work about five fifteen, and I walked with her back to her residence hall. It was a relief to be rid of the bag for the evening, even though it was more cumbersome than heavy. I had a crease in my shoulder from the strap, and I gratefully deposited the duffel bag on the floor beside an unmade bed in Judith's suite. The room wasn't much bigger than a large bathroom. There was barely enough room for two beds, two desks, and two dressers.

"I'll leave a note on the door for Mack that the bed's occupied," Judith said as she pulled off her sweater and headed to the second bedroom to change.

I did a double take. "Mack?"

"Yeah. Neat guy," she said over her shoulder. "I've known him for two years. He can fix any problem at all with a computer."

I tried not to appear shocked. It was like I was back at the University of Chicago. But after a night on Patrick's couch there, and after sharing a room with Les last night, I was ready for anything.

When Judith came into the common area of the suite again—the "living room"—she was wearing skintight jeans, ankle boots, and a low-cut jersey top. Her curly hair was hard to contain, and it didn't look as though she'd really tried. She ducked into the bathroom to put on mascara.

I wasn't even sure she knew my last name. How did she know that I wasn't a psycho with razor blades in my pocket or that I wouldn't sneak off during the night with all her stuff? I guess that with someone named Mack sleeping across from me, it was safe to conclude I wouldn't try.

"I'm going out with my guy tonight," Judith told me. "Make yourself at home—turn on the TV, whatever you want. If you go out, just leave the door unlocked. My own roomie's still out, and so is Mack. If you leave and can't get in the front entrance when you come back, ring the bell and I'll let my resident manager know to let you in. Bye."

I was tired from tramping around all afternoon with a bag over my shoulder. But it was a beautiful night, so I went for a walk around campus, careful to stay near people and not wander off in the shadows alone. I called Les on my cell and told him I had a place to crash. Then I got some ice cream, listened to a couple of guys playing guitars, and pretended I was a resident student like everyone else. As Les said, everyone would be strangers at first when I went to a new place. And then, little by little, a face would become a friend.

I got to bed about eleven thirty, tossed around a bit, and was just drifting off when I heard a door slam—the door to the living area. I heard a guy cough. Mack. Had to be.

I kept my eyes shut. I heard the knob turn on the door to our bedroom. Then a pause. He was reading Judith's note.

The handle turned more slowly. A rectangle of light fell on the floor, then his shadow as he came in and shut the door behind him. The tune to "Mack the Knife" played in my head.

Footsteps. I didn't even know these people. I didn't know whose bed I was staying in. Didn't know Judith, and I was sure I didn't know Mack.

I cleared my throat to let him know I was awake.

"How ya doin'?" said a male voice.

"Okay," I said. "How about you?"

"Great."

He kicked off his shoes. Left the room and went to the bathroom. I turned over to face the wall and pulled the covers up to my cheek. If a guy can find a stranger in his room and say, "How ya doin'?" he couldn't be so bad.

Next thing I knew, I woke once during the night. It was past four. Loud, steady breathing from Mack. The smell of his sneakers. When I woke again, it was going on eight. I got up, dressed, put my stuff together, and left a thank-you note for Judith. Les pulled up at our meeting place at a quarter past nine, and we were on our way.

"So where did you find a place to sleep?" Les asked me.

I casually leaned my elbow on the armrest. "Well, believe it or not, I lucked out and spent the night with a guy," I said.

I think Les lifted his foot off the gas because the car suddenly lost power, but then it picked up again, much more slowly.

"This . . . somebody you know?" he asked, and he sounded strange.

"I never saw him before," I said, trying to keep a straight face. "And I still don't know what he looked like. He just came in the room in the dark and . . ."

"*And?*"

I laughed. "Relax," I said. "He was my roommate. Separate beds. Somebody loaned me a bed for the night. The girl had gone home for the weekend. I guess you could say it's coed."

I could tell he felt better. "So how did you like the college?"

"It's okay. Fine, really. Two down, one to go."

It was a two-and-a-half-hour trip to George Mason, and by the time we got to Fairfax, I'd memorized the names of the football teams, the student newspapers, the famous former alumni, and the histories of all three colleges I was inspecting.

At this point Lester was more interested in getting back for the four o'clock Redskins game than he was in making sure I got a full dose of what George Mason was all about, so he gave me a whirlwind tour of the campus himself by car.

We did the Patriot Circle, following the map I'd printed out on the Internet. Then Les turned onto George Mason Boulevard and drove slowly around campus, all the little lanes between buildings.

From what I could tell from my printouts and from posters nailed about, Johnson Center was where all the action was on campus, and it was right in the middle, maybe the largest building next to the Field House. There were posters advertising jazz concerts in the JC Bistro, comedy shows, movies at the JC Cinema. . . .

But there's not a lot going on at a college campus at noon on a Sunday. A lone student here or there heading for a coffee shop; a faculty wife, maybe, pushing a stroller; a couple having an intense conversation near the George Mason statue.

Les waited while I checked out Fenwick Library, the student union, and the performing arts building. Then I got back in the car and said, "Let's go. Finished. Done!"

"Sure?" he asked.

"I'm saturated. I couldn't soak up another thing," I told him. "I've got a ton of homework waiting for me, and George Mason is close enough that I could drive over here for a second look by myself."

Les turned on the radio, and we headed back to the beltway toward Maryland. Les sang along with the music.

It wasn't really the way a college visit should go. I knew that. I knew that people like Gwen kept long lists of the pros and cons of various schools—scholarships, clubs, size, cost, dorms— while I had a manila folder and a couple of envelopes stuffed with whatever I got off the Internet, that and a few brochures.

But I liked William and Mary best, and it tied for first place with Maryland, which I'd visited several times with Les.

I liked the thought of going to the school that Jefferson had attended, but I also liked the thought of graduating from the same college as my brother and being closer to home. Maybe it was growing up without a mother that made me feel this way— like I needed an umbilical cord to *some*body.

I thanked Les when I got out of the car, pulled my duffel bag from the backseat and would swear I heard a relieved sigh as I closed the door and Les sped away.

I wondered if Dad and Sylvia had enjoyed having the house to themselves for the three-day weekend. No loud music coming from my bedroom; no bleary-eyed senior to look at over the breakfast table; no jacket on the back of a chair; no saucer left on an end table.

I walked through the living room and followed the sound of voices beyond the dining room and out to the high-ceilinged family room at the back of the house, where you could see the light yellow of the box elder's leaves through the windows.

The conversation seemed to stop in mid-sentence.

"Oh!" Sylvia said.

"Didn't think you'd be back until this evening," Dad said.

I realized by Sylvia's "Oh," by the redness of her eyes, and by the way they were sitting, Dad's arm around her, that she'd been crying. I didn't know what to do.

"We finished up early so Les could watch the game with his buddies," I said. "Am I interrupting something?"

"Not really," Sylvia said. She's no better at lying than I am.

"So how did things go?" Dad asked, extracting his arm from around Sylvia's shoulder and laying his hand on her knee instead.

"Okay. I got a good look at all three campuses, talked to some people," I said, wondering how to make a quick exit.

"Any of the three appeal?" Dad asked.

"I liked William and Mary the best," I said. "Anyway, I've got a ton of homework to do and some calls to make. . . ." I turned sideways to let them know I was leaving.

"There's some ham in the fridge," Sylvia said, and her nose sounded a bit clogged. "Some good cantaloupe, too."

"Thanks! I'll manage," I said.

I carried my duffel bag up to my room and dumped it on the bed. What was wrong? It hadn't looked like an argument. Not with Dad's hand on her knee. Sylvia didn't sound mad, she sounded sad.

Could Sylvia's sister in New Mexico be sick again? Her brother in Seattle? Was the Melody Inn going bankrupt and were we in danger of losing our house? My imagination had kidnapped my brain and was running away with it.

I spread my notebook and papers out on the bed and had just started my physics assignment when Sylvia tapped on the door and peeped inside.

"Got a minute?" she said.

"Sure." I put down my book and waited as she came in, hugging her bare arms in her short-sleeved sweater. It didn't seem that cold to me. She gave me an apologetic smile.

"I'm glad you had a good weekend, because mine was sort of crummy, and I just wanted you to know what Ben and I were talking about when you came in," she began.

Here it comes, I told myself. *Get prepared.*

"Remember the doctor's appointment I had last week?"

"I think so."

"Well, I had a routine mammogram, but I got a recall on it so I had to take it over. They've found something they want to check on a little further, and I have a biopsy coming up. I was feeling scared, that's all. Most biopsies turn out to be negative, but this is my first, so I was having a little cry, that's all."

That's all? I thought. Sylvia could have breast cancer and be operated on and she could die and Dad would go into this deep depression and wouldn't be able to work and he'd lose his job and I'd already lost one mother and . . . By the time Sylvia spoke again, I'd had us moved back to Chicago to live with Aunt Sally.

"Chances are that it's nothing, Alice, but I just hate waiting," she said. "I like to get things over with."

"Who doesn't?" I said. "When's the biopsy?"

"Week after next."

"And . . . when will you know? What it is?"

"I'm not sure. They have to send it to a lab and everything. I may be hard to live with until then, but it has nothing to do with you, and I just wanted you to know that. Ben's been wonderful. Other women go through a lot worse than this."

"Well, you can bitch all you like and I'll forgive you," I said, getting up and giving her a hug. "Thanks for letting me in on it. I hate not knowing what's going on."

"That makes two of us," she said. "Listen, I'm going to do some stir-fry later. Ben wants to watch the game, so we'll eat it in front of the TV at the half. With chopsticks!"

I smiled and she smiled, and I heard her footsteps going back downstairs.

For a moment or two I sat staring at the door of my room. My homework was there on the bed, the college stuff on my dresser, my duffel bag on the floor.

I got up and went over to my desk. I opened a drawer and took out my early admission form for the University of Maryland.

10

The Face of America

I ate dinner with Dad and Sylvia at the half—the Redskins were losing—but went back upstairs to finish the first part of the priority application and to tackle my homework.

The application didn't take long, actually. I didn't have to send in my transcripts, personal essay, and teacher recommendations till later— just a check for fifty-five dollars, the answers to four pages of questions, and Dad's signature.

During one of the commercial breaks, in the last quarter of the game when the Redskins had pulled ahead by three, I picked up the page where Dad had to sign, went back downstairs, got the checkbook from his desk, and took it to him.

"What's this?" he asked, putting down his coffee mug.

"I'm getting an early start on college applications," I said casually. "Just need your signature and a check for fifty-five dollars."

"Good for you," Dad said, taking the pen I handed him. "Which school?"

"U of Maryland," I said as the game came on again.

"Oh." He adjusted his glasses and took the checkbook, started to ask another question, but paused to watch the next play. "Watch that *def*ense!" he told the screen. Then he opened the checkbook. "I'll write the amount and sign it," he said. "You fill in the rest." He signed the application, too, where it said *Parent's Signature* and handed them both back to me. "There're only two minutes left of the fourth quarter, Al. You may want to watch," he said.

"Definitely," I told him. I took the big chair on the other side of the sofa. Sylvia sat curled up on the opposite chair, legs tucked under her. She wasn't looking so much at the screen as she was looking through it. Maybe all this was worse than she'd told me.

I made up my mind. I wasn't even going to apply to William and Mary. I wasn't going to apply to the University of North Carolina or George Mason. I would either commute back and forth to the University of Maryland, living at home where it was cheaper and where I could help Dad and Sylvia, however it turned out, or I wasn't going to college at all. I'd take a year off, work at the Melody Inn, and see them through this.

I hadn't told Dad a lie when I said I was starting to send out my college applications. I *was* starting out. I just wasn't finishing the rest, that's all.

We sent out two of our roving reporters to ask this question:

> WHAT, IF ANYTHING, MAKES
> YOU FEAR FOR YOUR SAFETY
> HERE AT SCHOOL?

> Mr. Samuels, if I don't find the
> keys to the chemistry cabinet.
> —Rod Ferguson, senior

> I feel pretty safe here. Especially
> with the security guards at the
> entrance and at games.
> —Steph Bates, sophomore

> Having to park a long way from
> school when there's a program at
> night.
> —Elissa Collins, senior

> Just the guys in the trench coats
> carrying the AK-47s.
> —Bud Batista, senior

My gym teacher.
—Charlie Ingram, freshman

This was Amy's second assignment as an *Edge* reporter, and one of the replies she brought in made us blink:

Besides the blacks and queers and Latinos who are polluting our schools and neighborhoods, you mean?
—Bob White, senior

"Omigod!" I said. "Pay dirt!"

The others looked up.

"Did I do it wrong?" Amy asked anxiously, hanging around to see if what she'd done was okay.

"You did well, Amy," I told her, and looked at the others. "Who's Bob White?"

Everyone else looked as blank as I did. I checked Amy's handwritten notes again. "He's a senior. Are you sure he said 'senior'?" I asked her.

She nodded. "I wrote it down just like he said it."

"What did he look like?" Phil wanted to know.

That's asking a lot of Amy. Facts she can handle; faces she can't. "Just a boy," she said.

"Was he tall?" someone asked her.

Amy looked up, then down, as though measuring something on the wall. She hunched her shoulders.

"Dark hair? Blond? Can you remember that?" Tim asked.

She swallowed.

"It's okay," I said. "We can look his picture up in the office. You did fine, Amy." And then, to Miss Ames, "But we can't print this, can we?"

Miss Ames turned toward the rest of us. "What do you think? There's nothing that says we have to print all the replies we get. . . ."

"I say we print it," said Phil. "My guess is that some kids are being targeted and aren't telling. There wouldn't be a Student Safety Council if there weren't. There wouldn't have been that incident in the hallway, or the double eights in Daniel's locker. If the victims aren't going to 'out' the group, maybe the newspaper can."

"I'll head for the office and look at student photos," said Sam.

Fifteen minutes later he was back to report that there was no student picture of Bob White because there was no Bob White registered in the school. We decided to print the reply along with all the others in the "Question of the Week" column, and Phil said he was going to write a special editorial to accompany it.

"And   maybe   we   should   start   a

letters-to-the-editor feature—like a sounding-off column—for people to express an opinion about it," I suggested. "That or anything else."

"Then let's call it that: 'Sound Off,'" said Phil.

"Except that some people don't know when to stop. It could take up the whole paper," said Tim.

"We'll reserve the right to edit letters as needed," Miss Ames said. "Full speed ahead."

The next morning Phil showed me a draft of his editorial:

IS THIS OUR FACE OF AMERICA?

We are a school of 1,600 in the shadow of the nation's capital. Our student body is somewhat transient, because many of our parents work for the government, and every two years the population shifts.

We are African American, Caucasian, Latino, Asian, and Native American. We are high school students, supposedly past the juvenile pranks of third and fourth grades and the thoughtless remarks of middle school. Yet in the past few weeks a student from Sudan has found a Nazi symbol in his locker and some armbands from the Gay/Straight Alliance were trashed. Someone using the pseudonym "Bob White" expresses racist views in our "Question of the Week" column. We published it because it was one answer to our question—and because it exposes a possible undercurrent of hate and intolerance on this campus. For a school that prides itself on our football team, our debate team, our band, our drama club and choir, is this *our* Face of America? Is this the best we can do?

—Phil Adler, Editor in Chief

Immediately following Phil's editorial was the headline SOUND OFF and this paragraph:

In future issues we will be devoting half a page to your letters to this paper. So that we may print as many letters as possible each issue, we ask that you keep them fairly short, no longer than 100 words. This is your chance to "sound off."

You may write about school, politics, religion, life in general, but we hope your comments will be honest reflections of how you feel. All letters must be signed. You can e-mail submissions to *The Edge*; you can slip them under the door of room 227; you could put them in our box in the office; you can even put a stamp on them and let the U.S. mail do the delivery. But whatever you have to say, we want to hear it. To start things off, we welcome your comments on Phil's editorial.

—Alice McKinley, Features Editor

A lot of possible replies to "Bob White's" racist comment were running through my head, but I had a lot to deal with at home. Sylvia was distracted and anxious over her scheduled biopsy . . . and angry at herself because she was.

"Every other woman I know has been through this, and it was nothing," I heard her say to Dad. "Why am I so upset by it?"

"Because it's happening to you and not some 'other woman,'" he said gently.

I heard her sigh. "I guess that's why I'm so sure that for me, it will be different. The results will be positive and I'll have to decide between a lumpectomy or chemo and I'll lose my hair and—"

"Good grief, you sound like Alice," said Dad, and there was a touch of impatience this time in his voice. He'd brought home some sales figures from the store, and they were lower than he'd expected for October. "Sylvia, do you have to borrow trouble? Can't we just deal with the problems we've got and not take on any more until we have to?"

I was silently placing dirty dishes from my room on the kitchen counter, but Sylvia was standing in the doorway between the living and dining rooms, and Dad was computing figures on the dining room table, so it was impossible for me not to hear.

"Two of my aunts had breast cancer, and one of my grandmothers died of it," she said. "I'm just plain scared."

Dad relented. I heard his chair squeak, then Sylvia's footsteps as she must have moved toward him.

"That's what makes you a good teacher." Dad's voice. "You look ahead, plan ahead, take all outcomes into account. I just try to keep my head above water. If it's cancer, we'll deal with it. Together. If it's not, then you're wasting some glorious autumn days worrying about it."

"What would I do without you?" Sylvia murmured, and I figured I needed to get back upstairs as noiselessly as I'd come.

We're not a rich family. Not even close. We aren't poor, either. We have a pretty nice house, now that we've remodeled, which Dad will be paying for for a long time. We have two cars, neither of them new. Les would graduate with his master's degree in December. But my tuition next year would take a huge chunk of our savings, I knew. Dad and Sylvia earned about the same, but they were both doing work they loved. The economy was down, however, and everyone knew it. I didn't understand the Dow Jones average in the newspaper, but I understood that there were a few more empty storefronts along Georgia Avenue.

Every time a store closed near the Melody Inn, it meant that those customers wouldn't be passing *our* store any longer. That there would be fewer people in *our* neighborhood. Maybe the owner of the Melody Inn chain would close Dad's store. Maybe Les would come back home to live. Maybe Sylvia would be too sick to teach and she'd lie in an upstairs bedroom and I'd have to give up dances and new clothes and my cell phone and . . .

I whacked myself on the cheek to bring me back to reality. *Think like Dad*, I told myself. *Don't expect trouble.* Except that there were signs of trouble brewing right there at school, and we didn't know where it was coming from or what would happen next.

I was on jury duty again that Wednesday. The accused was a girl who had been caught shoplifting—one of our sophomores. It would be her first offense, and the police, finding out that we had a Student Jury in our school, referred her to us to be disciplined.

She had already confessed and was both repentant and scared.

Darien asked her how her family had reacted to the news that she had shoplifted. Tearfully, she replied that her dad was furious with her, her mom had cried, and "my little brother doesn't look up to me anymore." Her voice trembled as she spoke.

"I'm really not like this," she said, seemingly shocked by her own behavior. "It was just . . . an impulsive thing. It's really not me."

We didn't have to discuss her case very long. We assigned her thirty hours of community service and sentenced her to write an essay about how the Student Jury experience would help her move toward her goal in life, which, she told us, was to be a wildlife photographer and a respected member of the community, not a criminal.

It was a beautiful October night with a full moon, and I went out back to sit on our screened porch after dinner. The scent of dry leaves made me think of hayrides and Halloween and the party back in junior high when Patrick French-kissed me in a broom closet.

I sat on the glider, a lap robe over my bare feet, a sweater around my shoulders, watching the moon rise higher and higher in the dark sky. On impulse I called Patrick on my cell.

"Heeey!" he said. "How *are* you? I was just thinking about you."

"Were you really?" I asked. "I was thinking about you too. In a broom closet."

"What?" There was laughter in his voice. "What's this about a closet?"

"Don't you remember? The French kiss?"

"You weren't supposed to know it was me! That's how I got up the nerve. It was dark!"

"Tell one friend, and you might as well broadcast it," I said. "Four different people told me it was you. What are *you* doing this evening?"

"Looking at the moon," he answered.

"You are? Right now?"

"I was. Coming back from dinner at the Medici. I found the initials you carved on the table."

I was delighted. "And the moon's full there too?"

"Of *course* it's full here. You never passed second-grade science?"

I laughed. "Okay, go to the window right now and look at the moon so I'll know we're both seeing it at the same time," I instructed.

His voice moved in and out, and I knew he was walking around. "Okay," he said. "I have to move my roommate's plant first."

"What kind of plant is it?"

"I don't know. His sister gave it to him to take to college. Looks sort of like a cornstalk, but shorter. Marijuana, maybe."

I laughed.

"I don't know what it is. He forgets to water it and the leaves are turning brown. Okay, I'm pulling up the blind . . . Oops. The cord's got a knot in it. Wait a minute . . ." Then he said, "It's gone."

"What's gone?"

"The moon. It's on the other side of the building."

"Go outside, Patrick! I want us both looking at the moon at the same time."

"Hold on." There was a five-second pause. "I'm going down the hall . . . I'm passing the room on the left . . . passing my roommate who's coming back from a movie. Hey, Jonah, water that freakin' cornstalk, would ya? . . . Okay, I'm turning a corner . . . going out the door . . . there are a lot of trees in the way. I've got to go out to the sidewalk . . . Ah! There it is! The moon! Now what?"

"Sit down somewhere and look at it, Patrick. Just think—we're both looking at the very same moon at the very same time. Like our eyes are almost meeting."

"Well, not quite, because you're seeing the east side of the moon there in Maryland and I'm seeing it from a Midwestern perspective."

"*What?*"

"If you measured the telescopic distance of the perimeter of the istobulus . . ."

"Patrick!"

"Okay. The moon is beautiful, and if I could see you, you are too. Where are you sitting? What are you wearing?"

"I'm on the back porch on the glider, wearing jeans and a red tee, with a lap robe over my bare feet."

"Then I'm kissing your toes," Patrick said.

I giggled.

"Want me to move up a little? Ankles? Knees?"

"Uh . . . I think Dad's on his way out here. I heard him pouring some coffee, and he usually brings it out here on the porch," I told him.

"That's okay. He can't see us. I'm kissing your knees now. That tender area just behind the knee—"

"He really *is* coming out here, Patrick! What am I going to say?"

"He can't see *me*."

"But he'll hear . . ." I laughed again as I heard Dad's footsteps cross the kitchen floor, the family room, and then the creak of the doorstep as he entered the porch.

"Now, I'm between your thighs . . . ," said Patrick.

"Oh! I didn't know you were out here," said Dad, sitting down in the wicker chair in one corner. Then, seeing my cell phone, he said, "Don't let me interrupt," and pointed to his iPod and earbuds. He leaned back with a satisfying sigh and lifted the cup to his lips, listening to the music and smiling up at the moon.

"Go on," I whispered to Patrick.

11

Letting Off Steam

We were beginning to get responses to Phil's editorial. Most had been stuck in the newspaper's box at the office:

> I think those things you
> mentioned happening were just
> jokes. Lighten up. I wouldn't
> know a Nazi if I saw one.
> > —Mark Hurley, junior

> It's really disturbing to me that
> this happened at our school.
> I want Daniel Bul Dau to
> know how glad I am to have
> him here.
> > —Gretchen Squire, freshman

> The only thing I can say for Bob
> White is that he's honest.

God help us.

—Craig Robinski, senior

But another letter was slipped under the door of the newsroom three days later:

What people don't realize is that this country is becoming a third world ghetto. We have a special club for homos. We make a black feel like a king just because he's from Africa; and the clerks in half the stores around school speak only Spanish. Pretty soon the whole United States will be a nation of mongrels. Don't say you weren't warned.

—Bob White, senior

"Oh . . . my . . . God!" said one of our junior reporters, one hand over her mouth.

"He's baaaaack!" said Phil.

"Who the heck *is* he?" said Sam. "It's driving me nuts!"

Phil looked over at me. "What do you think we should do with *this*?"

"Print it," I said. "I don't think too many people took the first one seriously."

We looked at Miss Ames. She nodded. "Print

it—just like it's written. But we're going to add an editorial note that says from now on, every letter has to be signed by a registered student. I'm hoping that sooner or later we'll smoke him out."

"But can you *believe* this?" said one of our sophomore reporters.

"I'd love to know this guy's story," Tim mused.

"Or not," said Sam.

I hated to have "Bob White's" comments resting uneasily on everyone's minds, though. If he found other kids who felt the same way he did—and he undoubtedly could—wouldn't this just encourage him?

Fortunately for us, Daniel handed me his feature article on life in Sudan the very next day. It fit in so perfectly with Phil's editorial of the week before that we redid the layout and cropped a couple photos to get it in:

> *Salaam 'alaykum.* I am writing Sudanese way of saying hello— "peace be upon you." Thank you for invitation to tell you about my life as Sudanese national.

> I am from Sudan with my mother and older brother. Geri is student at George Washington's University,

and we are having much gratitude to be in your country and give thanks to university for bringing my brother here to study. Also thanks to church for bringing my mother and myself, for how long, we are not sure. Here our mother helps cook in a restaurant her special Sudanese foods.

Things are very bad in my country right now. We have many tribes and many conflicts. There used to be music and dancing, but now in the place where we lived, women cannot dance with men even at weddings, and only religious music can be played for us on the radio. Many people have been killed, and when our village was burned, we ran all day and all night to get away.

Geri studies to be a lawyer so he can go back to Africa and change the government and help the people. I will study hard too, but it will not be easy to leave the United States of America if we are sent back. It is clean here and smells good, but I was a little much afraid before we came.

"You will get lost there," my friends said. "Don't get lost in America." I am careful not to lose myself. In refugee camp where we lived before we came, there was a school and I learned English. I can read your books and your street signs. In the U.S. of America there are so many streets that they are given letters and numbers. There is a First Street and a Fourteenth Street. There is an M and an R Street. Whoever saw so many streets?

You will understand that I had never been on an airplane. It crosses the ocean, and then it crosses the Potomac River. I ask my brother if there are crocodiles in the Potomac River. He doesn't know. The man beside him laughs. "No crocodiles," he says.

When I go back to Africa, I will tell my friends about the streets with numbers. About air-conditioning and machines that wash your clothes for you and microwave ovens that cook without fire. They will not believe me. And they will laugh when I tell them that in America, when it is warm, people seem to move about the streets in their underwear.

I will be glad to see my friends again if we go back to refugee camp. I miss hearing them laugh. I miss our games. But my brother does not think of these things. He loves America. He loves the rule of law, the elections, the jury system, and the hospitals with their clean floors.

Perhaps I will learn to love the U.S. of America as much as Geri does. Already I am liking the football here and the milk shakes and the chicken tenders that do not look like chickens. And I like that my mother sings.

—Daniel Bul Dau, senior

• • •

With all the budget cuts that had happened during the year, food banks and area shelters were really hurting. So at Halloween our school, along with the teen center and some of the neighborhood churches, announced that high school students would be trick-or-treating for donations—canned food or monetary donations—in place of candy. We had to register first, of course, and get an official collection can, but we loved any excuse to put on crazy outfits.

Four of us decided to dress up as food product emblems, which took a lot more time and glue than we'd imagined. Gwen had found a peanut costume at a secondhand store and, with a top hat, became Planters' Mr. Peanut. Pamela turned herself into the Jolly Green Giant. Liz was either Betty Crocker or Sara Lee, she couldn't decide which. And I dressed up like the Quaker Oats man—with a broad-brimmed black hat, a ruffled shirt under my chin, and holding a Quaker Oats box with the contribution can inside it.

"*Look* at you!" I squealed as Pamela arrived with green tinted skin and a sort of leaf-stitched tunic around her. It was Gwen who was funniest, though—the top half of her encased in a papier-mâché peanut shell, arms sticking out holes in the sides, and her legs in beige-colored tights. We had a great time going house to house, trolling for contributions, bringing whole families to the door to admire us.

It had been warm during the afternoon but grew colder after the sun went down. We'd got a late start, and though we often collided with groups of little kids at the start of the evening, we'd forgotten that porch lights usually went off around nine, signaling that the owners were shutting down.

We kept at it for another half hour and were about to head back to my place, where Gwen had parked, when Keeno drove up with a friend from St. John's.

"I don't believe this!" he called when he recognized Liz. "I thought it was a party you were going to. You're doing all this for *candy*?"

Liz and I raised our containers and rattled the money.

"Oh, man," said his friend. "Streetwalkers!" We laughed.

Keeno introduced us to the heavyset guy in the red St. John's sweatshirt. "Louie Withers," he said. "Soccer player."

We stood under a streetlight talking, and the guys tried to guess our costumes. They got Mr. Peanut, the Quaker Oats guy, and the Jolly Green Giant, but they had a little trouble with Elizabeth's outfit.

"Little Miss Muffet?" Keeno guessed.

"Bo Peep?" asked Louie.

"You flunk," said Liz. "No brownies for you."

We said we'd tell them if they would drive us to the Italian sandwich shop on University Boulevard, so that's where we ended up.

"So who *are* you?" Louie asked Liz when we got to the shop.

"Betty Crocker," she told them as we squeezed into the largest booth and Gwen removed her peanut top, revealing a T-shirt beneath.

"Huh? The woman who sewed the flag?" asked Louie, and we shrieked.

"That was Betsy Ross, moron," said Keeno. "Jeez, turn your sweatshirt inside out, will you? The headmaster would have a heart attack."

It turned out that the guys had been supervising a neighborhood Halloween party where Keeno had played his guitar with a funky band. We were all pretty ravenous and ate the freshly-made calzones, washed down with Sprite and Pepsi.

"I'm sweltering," I said, removing the black velvet jacket I'd borrowed from Sylvia.

"I'm freezing," said Pamela, her green shoulders bare. "Let me wear that."

"Not if you get green color on it," I warned. "It's Sylvia's."

"I know where you could get cool and Pamela could get warm, and it's free," said Keeno.

"Don't listen to any of his ideas," I warned

the others. "Remember Tombstone Tag?"

"Cemetery Tag," Liz corrected.

"What the heck is that?" asked Louie.

"A way to get the cops on you," said Pamela.

"No, I'm serious. This'll be fun," said Keeno.

What's that old adage? *Fool me once, shame on you; fool me twice . . .*

Like lemmings, we got up, paid our bill, and followed Keeno out to his car. It was already after eleven, but we were up for anything.

"How far is it? Another state?" asked Liz.

"Nope," said Keeno. "Couple more blocks, in fact. The only thing you have to remember is that nobody talks or laughs out loud."

"Uh-oh," said Gwen.

The car slowed. Keeno turned onto a side street and parked next to an alley. "Keeno . . . ," I said, giggling.

"We're not hurting anything," he assured us, getting out. "Trust me."

"Right," said Pamela. "Where have we heard that before?"

Still, we followed him into the alley, sticking close to the high fence that separated the back-yard from the garbage cans, our bodies bent at the waist like cops closing in on a suspect.

When we came to the first driveway, Keeno stopped. "Now you don't have to take your clothes off unless you want to—"

"*What?*" said Gwen.

"Shhhh," Keeno cautioned. "I've been here before. Just remember to whisper."

Despite our better judgment, we moved up the driveway, setting each foot down carefully. A thin veil of clouds moved across the moon, making it difficult, but not impossible, to see in the darkness. Straight ahead, on the back of the house, we could just make out a sign reading GUEST PARKING ONLY.

"Keeno, what *is* this?" I whispered, grabbing his arm.

And then I saw the second sign: PINEVIEW BED-AND-BREAKFAST.

"Omigod!" Liz whispered.

"I'm freezing!" Pamela whimpered.

The breeze had picked up. In a half hour or so it would be November, and I had mailed the first part of my application to the U of Maryland that morning. Maybe I deserved a little celebrating.

One finger to his lips, Keeno led us across the yard and into the shelter of a couple trees— evergreens, of course—and pointed to something attached to the back porch. A hot tub.

"Oh, no!" I heard Gwen whisper.

"You've got to be kidding," said Liz.

"What's wrong?" he whispered back. "It's wonderful! You should try it."

"You're out of your mind," said Gwen. "How

do you know it's hot? How do you even know there's water in it?"

"Because they keep it hot year-round. It's in their advertisement," Keeno said. "Trust me. I've used it in the middle of February."

"They'll catch us!" said Liz.

"Not if we're quiet, they won't. Look." He pointed up to the dark windows. "No guests. The parking lot's empty and the lights are off."

"So who goes first?" asked Pamela, hugging herself.

"We'll go," said Keeno. "Just don't take long and don't make a sound."

We pretended not to look as the guys took off their shoes and slipped out of their jeans and jackets. But we stared wide-eyed, hands over our mouths to suppress the laughter, as we watched two naked bottoms go streaking across the short stretch of lawn to the porch steps, ascend in the darkness, then disappear at the other end.

"I can't believe we're doing this," said Liz. "Can't we undress on the porch?"

"With the guys watching us from the water?" said Pamela. "C'mon. Strip. My arms are like ice." She slipped out of her Jolly Green Giant costume, and the rest of us started undressing. Leaving our clothes in a little heap under the trees, we carefully made our way across the yard in our bare feet, then hurried silently up the steps, and across the darkened porch. One at a time, with the guys offering outstretched hands to help us down, we slid into the hot water and sank down to chin level, savoring the warmth. There we were, six floating heads in the darkness, with just enough moonlight to make out each other's faces.

"Keeno, this is your best idea yet!" I whispered as my toes touched someone in the middle of the large tub.

"I wish we could turn the motor on," Pamela whispered.

"Yeah, but they'd hear it, and the controls are inside," said Keeno.

The water was so deep that I was only half sitting. My bottom kept lifting off the seat and my legs floated effortlessly, tangled up now and then with other legs, our heads resting on the indentations around the rim, knees touching, side to side. "We could do a water ballet," Liz whispered.

"What would we call ourselves? The Naked Six?" asked Louie.

We muffled our laughter and watched the clouds pass over the face of the moon. It was a little weird being in a hot tub without the hum of the motor, the swish of the water, the force of the jets. Like being in a bathroom together with no background music.

"Down!" Keeno hissed suddenly as a car turned into the alley, its headlights sweeping the back of the house and moving rapidly toward us. Instantly, all six of us submerged and rose up only when we ran out of air. The car had moved on and turned in someone else's driveway farther on. We wiped the water from our eyes and settled back again.

"Whose knee keeps poking mine from across the tub?" asked Pamela. "Keeno's, I'll bet. I swear, guys' knees are like ice picks. All angles and points."

"And girls' knees," said Keeno, one hand on Liz's knee, "are like soft, velvety, uh . . ." His hand was obviously kneading her flesh and moving slightly up the thigh. Liz laughed and pushed his hand away, and we unanimously cautioned her to be quiet.

We played footsies under the water and took turns being It—another of Keeno's ideas, obviously. With all of our feet together on the bottom, the "it" person would choose one foot in particular and, by examining it with his own two feet, try to guess whose foot it was.

I was It. I chose a foot and clasped it between my own. It could have been either a large girl's or a small guy's foot. High arch, I could tell that much.

"Somebody needs to cut his toenails," I whispered, and soft giggles traveled around the group. I pushed the foot up on its heel and ran the big toe of my other foot along its bottom. The foot immediately twitched and pulled back. "Ah! Ticklish, are we?" I whispered, and tickled some more. I saw Liz give her leg a jerk and immediately chose her. We laughed.

"Hey, hey! Keep it down!" Keeno whispered. "Shhhh." We submerged again up to our lips, looking in all directions, but no lights came on, no door opened on the porch.

"What time is it?" Pamela wanted to know.

"I don't know. Left my watch in my jeans," said Louie.

"What's this?" asked Gwen. She held up a flip-flop. "Did somebody wear flip-flops in here?"

"I did," said Pamela. "I forgot to take them off."

"Maybe we'd better head out pretty soon," whispered Keeno. "I don't want to press our luck."

"Where's my other flip-flop?" asked Pamela.

"Find it before we leave, or we're toast," said Louie.

We all felt around to see if it was caught behind us or floating under our legs. My hand touched something, but it sure wasn't a flip-flop, and Louie looked at me in surprise. "Sorry," I said, and felt heat rising in my face.

Pamela found the flip-flop on the bench behind her, and we agreed to get going.

Keeno rose up and looked all around. When

there were no stirrings from indoors that we could see, no lights coming on or off, he whispered to Louie, "Let's go." They got out, backsides showing up white in the darkness, quickly climbing the steps out of the tub and onto the porch, then down the stairs on the other side, where they darted across the lawn and into the shelter of the trees.

"Omigod, you know what I grabbed?" I told the others as soon as the guys were gone. "I was looking for Pamela's flip-flop and took hold of Louie's . . ." We covered our mouths and submerged for a second to stifle our laughter.

"This was wild!" said Liz. "Leave it to Keeno."

"We've gotta go," said Pamela. "It's going to feel like forty when we get out."

"Gotta do it," said Gwen. "No squealing. Ready? One . . . two . . . three."

One by one we followed her up the steps to the porch, our feet making contact with the wood planks. It occurred to us only then that there were no fluffy towels waiting to envelop us, no towels at all. And at that exact moment, another car came toward us on the side street and slowed at the entrance to the alley.

We stopped dead still. Gwen put out her arms to keep us from going any farther as the car turned and its headlights moved across the back of the house. We might as well have been onstage because the spotlight shone on each one of us in turn.

Worse yet, the minute the headlights had reached the last cowering girl, the car suddenly braked, then started backing up. With little shrieks, we went racing down the steps. The headlights swept over the back porch again, but this time we were gone. Finally the car went on down the alley and pulled in somewhere else.

I don't know whose jeans I yanked on there in the cluster of trees. The guys kept handing us pieces of clothing, and we pulled them on as fast as we could. Gwen had worn tights under her peanut costume, but her legs were too wet to pull them on. She pulled on her underwear and a guy's sweater, and as soon as we could, we were running down the alley to Keeno's car.

"My jacket!" I cried. "Has anybody got my jacket?"

"Hurry up!" Louie was saying, holding the car door open.

No one had the jacket.

"I've got to go back!" I said. "It's Sylvia's!"

"Cripes, Alice!" said Keeno.

I was only half dressed—my jeans and bra. Somebody else had my shirt. I raced back up the driveway and into the cluster of trees, my eyes searching for a heap of black velvet.

My heart was pounding as I moved around the base of the trees, around the parking lot, scanning the ground. I exhaled in relief when I found the jacket against the trunk of a tree, and I swooped it up and ran back across the parking lot.

"Hey!" came a man's voice, and suddenly the porch light came on. Not only the porch light, but a floodlight illuminating the whole guest parking area.

"Hey!" the man yelled again. "You're trespassing, you know. Who the hell are you?"

"I'm sorry," I called timidly over my shoulder, but I didn't stop.

Liz was waiting for me in the alley. She grabbed my arm, and we ran as though dogs were after us. Keeno had the engine running when we reached the car, and we tumbled inside, shrieking.

I expected to hear footsteps coming after us. The wail of sirens, even.

But Keeno turned at the next corner, then again at the light, and we screeched and laughed as we melted into the traffic and cruised innocently along the street. Our hair was dripping water all over the place, and we used someone's fleece jacket to dry our heads, passing it from one to the other.

"Omigod, my heart's still thumping," I said, panting. "I was sure the owner would catch me."

"I'll bet the neighbors called him," said Louie. "Bet that last driver in the alley told him that some kids were goofing around in his hot tub."

"Relax, already!" said Keeno. "We didn't hurt anything."

"Yeah, but we can't go back there again. He's onto us," said Louie.

"Funny you never invited *us* here before," said Liz.

"Never knew you wanted to get naked before," said Keeno, and we all broke into laughter.

"Man, though, he almost nailed you," Louie said, turning around and looking at me.

"Yeah, he could have had a camera and taken your picture for evidence," said Keeno. "There it would be on the Metro page of the *Post*: 'Senior Arrested for Trespassing'!"

"Well, the *Gazette*, maybe," said Gwen.

"How about 'Features Editor of High School Newspaper Caught Nude'?" said Pamela.

"No, I've got it," said Liz. "'Member of Student Jury to Be Tried by Her Peers.' How's that for the next headline in *The Edge*?"

Nothing could ruin this evening, though. A perfect way to start November.

12

Incident Number Three

The same day *The Edge* published "Bob White's" mongrelization comment and Daniel's essay, the local news reported four separate incidents of tire slashing in Latino neighborhoods, and on all the rims, the letters *HH* had been chalked. None of the incidents took place near our school, but on Friday, Mr. Beck's voice came over the sound system:

"Good morning, students. It's not customary for me to intrude on your news and announcements, but I have something important to say. Yesterday there were several instances of tire slashing in our community, and most of you are aware of a couple of hate-inspired incidents in our school as well. Two recent comments in *The Edge*, by a student using a pseudonym, serve as another example of the kind of prejudice that provokes vandalism or worse. I was glad to read that in the future no letters will be published unless the author can be identified.

"I am not suggesting that anyone in this school is responsible for the tire slashing. And I know by your letters to *The Edge* that most of you do not hold similar views as those of the anonymous student.

"We are proud of our ethnic diversity. The fact that there are at least thirty-one different countries represented in our school provides us with a cultural richness that enhances your education, not diminishes it. This school will always stand for the free expression of ideas and concerns, but we will not tolerate bullying, vandalism, violence, or racial slurs.

"To students of every race, nationality, religion, or sexual orientation, we promise that we will do our utmost to protect you and your rights in this country. To those who would like to express a difference of opinion, no matter how unpopular it may be, we invite you to engage in respectful dialogue. We do not prosecute students just because they might have different views on politics or social issues. But we do expect responsible behavior of high school students. Demand this of yourselves and of your friends, and make this school proud."

We noticed that another security guard was added to the two regulars, and Mr. Gephardt was very visible as he talked with students one-on-one in the hallways.

Earlier in the week Miss Ames had asked me

to check out the Student Safety Council to see if we could get any leads on who else might be feeling intimidated here at school. Maybe do a write-up of how the council got started. Were students worried about what had happened at Columbine and Virginia Tech? Were they being harassed out in the parking lot or on the buses? Surely this wasn't just a look-both-ways-before-crossing-the-street kind of club. So I'd checked the activities calendar and saw that the SSC met on Fridays at 3:15 in G-108. That was forty-five minutes after classes were officially over.

That very day after school I did a little reading, listening to the hustle and shouts outside growing dimmer and dimmer as the buses rolled away. Gradually the parking lot emptied too, until finally there were only occasional footsteps in the hall, the close of a book, or the scooting of a chair to interrupt the quiet. At 3:05, I put my stuff in my bag, took out a small notebook, and headed down the main hall to the stairs.

There was band practice at the far end of the building. I could barely hear it as I descended the stairs, and by the time I reached the ground level, it had faded entirely.

I checked the number of one of the classrooms. Wrong hallway. Taking the first cross corridor, I passed the furnace room, the boiler, the custodian's office, then listened for conversation as I reached the second hallway. The science labs and photo studio, with their chemical smells, sat side by side along this corridor. Mine were the only footsteps on the tiled floor.

I found G-108, and it was empty. I went inside and turned on the light. I was still five minutes early. From all appearances, it seemed to be a freshman earth science room. A bulletin board had photos of a recent volcanic eruption in various stages, and a plastic model of the earth's layers sat on a side table.

I sat down in a chair near the back and surveyed a large maple tree outside the window. It had shed half its leaves, and with each gust of wind, a few more peach-colored leaves let go and swirled, forsaken, to the ground.

When another five minutes had gone by and no one came, I wondered if they had been scared off. It occurred to me that I hadn't seen Curtis Butler at our last GSA meeting either. Who else besides Daniel had gotten a warning logo? Who else might have had their cars vandalized and were afraid to report it?

Down the hall, the huge furnace cut on and off with clicks and swooshes. The hallway outside the room suddenly grew darker as the after-hours lighting went into effect. Outside, the sun emerged from behind some clouds, then receded. The wind blew, then calmed, then gusted again, as though the weather couldn't commit. The room seemed colder.

"You waiting for somebody?"

I jumped as a figure appeared in the doorway. One of the custodians poked his head inside.

"I thought the Student Safety Council was meeting today," I told him.

"Don't look like nobody's coming. I got to do this floor," he said.

"Come on in, I'm leaving," I said. "Maybe I've got the time mixed up."

He waited, swish broom ready, as I gathered my things and headed back to the stairs.

The office was open till four, so I went back and asked one of the administrative assistants, "Safety Council? No one was there."

"That's what I've got," she said, checking her calendar. "Fridays, three fifteen to four fifteen, G-108. Mr. Bloom is faculty adviser."

"Civics teacher?"

"Yes. Gordon Bloom. He was just in here a minute ago. I'll bet he's on the way to his car."

I used the faculty door, and sure enough, he was about twenty feet ahead of me, unlocking his station wagon.

"Mr. Bloom?" I called, and he paused as I ran over. "I'm doing an article for *The Edge* and wanted to mention the Safety Council, but no one was at the meeting."

"Oh, sorry about that," he said. "It's been scratched. I'll tell Betty to take it off the calendar."

"Why? Not enough members or what?" I asked. "Was there some particular problem they were concerned about?"

"To tell the truth, it was hard to put your finger on it," he said, smiling genially. "And I didn't make every meeting." He put his briefcase on the backseat, then rested his arms on the roof of the wagon. "There didn't appear to be any one issue exactly . . . just . . . a general uneasiness, I'd call it. Not a big group . . . five guys and two girls. But it seemed their focus was going to be on martial arts—protecting themselves, I guess—and I had to disband it."

"Why?"

"It was kids teaching kids. We're not insured for that. I told them they'd have to get their training somewhere else by a professional. Maybe talk with a P.E. instructor about starting a class." He smiled again. "Sorry, but I have to pick up a daughter from a dance class. Gotta scoot."

"Thanks," I told him, and headed for Sylvia's car over in student parking.

General unease. Self-protection. Martial arts. What did those students know that the rest of us didn't? *Who* was intimidating them? Could the majority of the student body be so out of touch that we didn't even know what was going on in our own school? Never an idea of what was going on until it happened?

Gwen and Pam and Liz and I took in a movie that night—anything to get away from the grind at school. I found that the easiest way I could use either Dad's or Sylvia's car was to offer to fill the tank and wash the windshield. They let me use their credit cards, of course, but hated the chore of having to stop at a station.

I picked up my friends early so I could get gas on the way. After I'd inserted the credit card in the slot, I was surprised when Liz got out of the car and asked if I could show her how to pump gas. Her dad usually filled their tank himself.

"In case I ever run low and have to do it," she said.

"You want to take over?" I asked, unscrewing the gas cap. She warily studied the hose and nodded.

"Okay," I told her. "After you take back your credit card, follow the instructions on the screen."

Lift handle, it read.

Gingerly, Liz grasped the handle with both hands.

Lift latch.

"Where?" she asked, looking around. I pointed. She flipped up the latch.

"Now put the nozzle in the opening."

Suddenly gasoline started squirting out the nozzle, all over the pavement.

"It's coming!" Liz shrieked, jumping backward.

"Don't squeeze, Liz!" I yelled. "Stop squeezing!"

Gwen and Pamela piled out of the car, screaming with laughter as Elizabeth dropped the hose on the ground like a hot potato, and the flow stopped.

"You have to wait till you get it in," Gwen hooted as customers turned to look.

"I'm terrified of that thing," Liz said.

"Don't squeeze till you get the nozzle inside," I told her. "Pick it up and push it all the way in, but *don't* squeeze yet!"

Liz bent down and picked up the hose, holding it as far away from her as possible. She moved over to the gas tank and thrust the nozzle down inside.

"Now," I said, "squeeze the handle."

Liz's fingers clamped down hard. "Nothing's happening," she said. I looked up at the pump window. No figures moving across the screen.

"Are you squeezing?" asked Pamela, barely able to get the words out, she was laughing so hard. Liz's anxious concentration made it all the funnier.

"As hard as I can," said Liz.

"Let up and squeeze slowly this time," I said.

"Awk! It's coming! Take it, Alice!" she said.

"What?" I grabbed the nozzle before she could pull it out, and Liz jumped back.

"What's wrong?"

She backed up against the pump. "It's too embarrassing!"

"Embarrassing?" I asked.

"So . . . so *phallic!*" she cried. *"Put it in. Squeeze! Don't squeeze. Squeeze harder! Squeeze slower!"*

We exploded with laughter. When a young attendant came over and asked if he could help, we could only shake our heads and wave him on.

When Gwen finally caught her breath, she said, "Only one thing to do, girl. It comes natural to guys. Get Keeno to show you how."

My AP English teacher was sick for three days, and Dennis Granger filled in for her. There was sort of this unspoken feeling of . . . I don't know. Uneasiness? Excitement, even? Cautiousness? Like I couldn't be entirely comfortable around him. I wasn't the only one either, and he wasn't the first or only teacher who had made me feel this way. It was just that among girls, when we said his name, it was our tone of voice, the accent on *Granger*, that signaled to each other, *Oh, that guy! Watch it!*

He was always finding a reason, it seemed, to reach over us or around us. If his arm brushed against my breast, I'd think, *Did I just imagine that because he's so handsome?* If I thought his hand grazed my butt as I passed his desk and I turned to look, his attention was somewhere else, and I'd think, *That didn't happen.*

Yet it was the kind of thing you didn't talk about seriously with your friends for fear they'd say, or think, *You wish!* We didn't cluster around him, though, like we did with some of our favorite teachers. We each made sure we weren't the last girl out of the classroom. And what could we report, even? *He might have brushed my breast? He possibly touched my butt? He was undressing me with his eyes, I think?* Right.

It was a day after gym class that I got the vibes. We'd played a hard game of volleyball, and there was a line at the water cooler before we went to the showers. I decided to wait. But later, as I left the gym, I realized I still hadn't had a drink, so I headed to the fountain in the west corridor. Someone was ahead of me, and I waited until she was through, then eagerly bent over the machine, filling my mouth with the ice-cold stream, then swallowing it down, filling up again, my throat welcoming gulp after gulp.

I felt someone waiting behind me, and then I felt something else. Pressure, hardness, just for a moment. And when I straightened up and turned, Dennis Granger smiled and said, "Excuse me," and leaned over the fountain as I quickly moved aside.

That was no accident, I told myself as I walked on to my next class. I felt I was blushing, but there was no one to see. He didn't follow, didn't call out to me, but just knowing that I turned him on, that he . . . what? . . . must have found me attractive, made me feel . . . confused. Ashamed, sort of, I don't know why. Even excited. I hugged myself and felt a shiver. *The three Cs*, I told myself. *When you're not Comfortable with it, it's not a Compliment, it's Creepy.* Yet how do you walk into the office and say, *I want to report a teacher who stood too close to me at the fountain*? You don't. I didn't, anyway.

Just stay five feet away from him at all times, I thought, and was glad my English teacher was coming back the following day.

Christmas comes practically the day after Halloween—for merchants, anyway. As soon as the witches and black cats come down, the angels and Santas move in, and Thanksgiving gets lost in the middle. Step in any store the first of November and you'll be surrounded by twinkly lights and "I wonder as I wander . . ." over the sound system.

We're always late making the switchover

at the Melody Inn. Because we have so many schoolkids trooping in for music lessons in the upstairs soundproof booths, we do Halloween up big, with fake cobwebs over the grand piano, black cats with arched backs protecting the sale table, and a life-size witch doll sitting on a stool by the front door.

In years past Dad declared that November should be dedicated to Thanksgiving. But this year, with sales down and stores closing on Georgia Avenue, we went right to Christmas. I spent one Sunday morning arranging a Christmas window display while Dad and Marilyn, in coats and scarves, stood out on the sidewalk and indicated whether I was to move the Christmas tree to the right or left and where to put the puppy.

It had taken three men to roll the piano up a ramp and into the display window. The scene we were trying to create—one of several that came from corporate headquarters—was of a happy family opening gifts from the Melody Inn on Christmas morning. The mom mannequin we'd rented was seated on the piano bench, wrapped in a blue silk shawl on which a score from the "Moonlight" Sonata was reproduced. The dad wore a sweatshirt with a profile of Beethoven on the front.

My job was to maneuver myself around this display in my stocking feet, trying to fit a teenage mannequin in place, holding a music box with a dancing fox on her lap, surrounded by more Melody Inn gift boxes, as well as a baby, sucking on a pacifier, crawling about in his little Santa Claus pj's. There wasn't a lot of space, and it seemed that every time I'd get one thing right, it accidentally threw something else off balance. The baby pajamas that came with the rented set were a size too small, however, and I struggled to make them fit. But Marilyn's nose was pink with cold and her coat wouldn't button all the way over her growing belly, so Dad sent her back inside and finally, when I was down to the small details, he came back in too.

We're usually closed on Sundays, but for the Christmas season we were now open from eleven to five, and I hurried to get things set up for my regular stint in the Gift Shoppe. When I returned to the main showroom at last, Dad turned on the twinkly lights that rimmed the display window and put in a CD of madrigal music.

"Hope it sells loads of pianos, Mr. M.," Marilyn said.

Kay came in a few minutes later, and when Dad unlocked the door at eleven, there were already four people waiting.

We were busy from the get-go. A father came in to buy a guitar for his son; someone wanted to mail an accordion to Kansas. I was gift wrapping a coffee mug for a customer when Kay noticed some people standing outside the window laughing. More people stopped. They laughed too.

"Now what?" said Dad. "Al, check the display window, would you?"

I walked to the front of the store and saw nothing unusual so I went outside. The tightly stretched pajama bottom of the baby had slipped down his plaster body, and there he was, mooning the shoppers out on their holiday errands.

Things were getting more complicated at home. My decision to go to the University of Maryland so I could be here for Dad and Sylvia was being severely tested. Sylvia, in fact, had good news. She had just received the results of her biopsy of the week before and the test was negative, she announced to Dad and me when we got home on Monday. Her smile was one hundred percent genuine. On Sylvia, you can tell.

Dad gave her a bear hug and rocked her back and forth. "*Wonderful* news, sweetheart," he said into her ear.

"The radiologist wants me back in six months for a sonogram, just to check, but she said everything looks perfectly normal."

"Dinner out?" I said hopefully.

"I don't know why not!" said Sylvia, and out we went.

Well then, maybe I should *apply to the other colleges*, I thought. I needed a "safe" school, and that would be Maryland. Once again the thought of a whole new place, a new roommate, difficult courses, and possibly unsupportive professors— all happening to me at the same time—brought back some of that panicky feeling. But I thought of myself at William and Mary, walking to class with someone like Judith, walking on a brick side- walk thinking of Jefferson and eating Moroccan chicken in the caf. I could do that.

So when we got back, I fished two more applications from the heap and began.

13

Call to Aunt Sally

November is one of the dreariest months. It hits you on the day you realize that all the leaves have fallen and everything is gray—the trees, the sky, the ground. Even people look gray. Which is why the seventh-period assembly the following week was so much fun.

There's an organization that sponsors amateur actors—teens and college age—who emphasize responsible sexual behavior. They put on awareness-based shows at high schools, focusing on issues like abstinence, birth control, HIV, prenatal development. . . . Each show has a number of skits, and they're just goofy enough to keep our attention.

The skit I liked best had a guy with a long curvy tail playing the part of a sperm, and a girl, sitting in a large cardboard oval, playing the egg. Emphasizing that it takes both to make a baby, the sperm darts carefree about the stage, chanting, "Sperm alone, no baby," while the girl files her nails and chants, "Egg alone, no baby." But when the sperm finds himself drawn into her orb, she wraps them both up in her blanket, and they emerge holding a doll between them.

Then, to show that both are responsible for bringing up this child if they make a baby, they do a frantic pantomime where he's feeding the baby while she's changing its diaper, then he does the diapering and she feeds the baby, at fast speed. A voice announces that condoms are free from Planned Parenthood, and the skit ends with the couple singing a parody of "Don't Worry, Be Happy," renamed "Don't Hurry, Use Condoms." I guess you'd have to be there.

We've had assemblies like this before, and like this one, the actors are kids our own age, and the group's purpose—"to inform, entertain, and educate"—is easy to swallow.

Some of the other skits were about eating disorders, body image, sexual abuse, suicide, rape, teen pregnancy—any personal thing that affects our lives.

Okay, so maybe most of us already knew the facts about this stuff—it wasn't old hat. But Jill, sitting behind me with Justin, got on my nerves.

One of the actresses was stating the reasons she'd decided to be celibate until she married. Jill, in particular, was whispering and giggling, mimicking the girl. The actress wasn't being preachy or anything—just saying that for her, abstinence seemed best. Jill obviously found it hilarious. It was especially annoying because I was trying to take notes so I could write up the program for the newspaper, and I missed some of the lines.

"Hey, Jill, knock it off, would you?" I whispered over my shoulder.

There were a few seconds of silence, then sputtering laughter from Jill.

"Quiet, everybody. Alice is learning something here," she responded in a stage whisper, and got a few, but only a few, titters in response.

Later, when Jill began laughing again, I heard Justin say, "Shhhh," and I wondered, for maybe the hundredth time, what—other than her absolutely gorgeous body—he saw in her.

Amy Sheldon liked the show, though. She must have been sitting near Jill too because afterward she said to me, "I don't know why some people didn't like it. It was just facts. You shouldn't be afraid of facts, my dad says."

"And he's absolutely right," I told her.

"Except sometimes people use facts to fool you," she went on. "Some people call me a retard, and that isn't true. You can be good in some things and slow in other things, and I'm very good at memorizing lists. My mom says

I'm the best memorizer she's ever seen. So does my tutor."

"You have a tutor? What subject?"

"Literature. I'm good at memorizing the characters' names and everything, but I don't always understand the story. The theme, I'm not so good with at all. But I like facts."

It was good to see Amy broadening herself, connecting more with other people. And I noticed she wore her *Edge* reporter badge even when she wasn't doing an assignment. *Whatever works*, I thought.

It was also good to see the number of letters coming in for the "Sound Off" section of our paper, and we included the few that responded to "Bob White's" latest comment:

> I'll bet B.W. doesn't even go to our school. I've never heard anyone else talk like that.
> —Caroline Eggers, sophomore

> How does he think *he* got to this country? Does he know where *his* ancestors came from? Every one of us came from somewhere else.
> —Mary Lorenzo, senior

I thought Hitler died in 1945. Let's
not resurrect him here.
—Cindy Morella, senior

This is America, "Bob White." Get
over it.
—Peter Oslinger, senior

Mostly, I think, his letter was ignored. There
were dozens of other items to interest the reader.
The newspaper staff couldn't ignore him, though.
We kept mulling it over at staff meetings.

"Who the heck do you think he is—one of
the jocks?" someone wondered.

"Or *she* is. Or *they*!" I said.

"Whoever they are, they evidently scared the
Safety Council right out of the school," said Phil.

"Into the martial arts, anyway," I said.

"I'll bet it's one of the Goths," said a sophomore roving reporter. "Nobody wants to take on
the Goths."

Amy Sheldon came in just then, flustered
because she was late but wanting to fit into the
conversation. "Some boys on the bus say bad
things," she said.

"Like what?" asked Phil.

"Like calling people names."

"Do you know who they are?" he asked.

Amy shook her head.

"What kinds of things do they say?" asked Sam.

"One of them said, 'What do you get if you mix a retard with a Latrino?' And the answer was 'A clogged toilet.' I don't understand it, but I told it to Dad, and he said it wasn't even funny."

"And stupid besides," I told her.

Miss Ames pulled last year's yearbook from a shelf and turned to the student pictures of each class. She handed the volume to Amy and said, "Do you think if you looked over the photos, you could recognize any of the boys who were talking like that? We can skip the seniors, because they're gone."

"And this year's freshmen aren't even in that yearbook," said Phil.

I knew this would be too hard for Amy. But she dutifully scanned picture after picture of juniors, sophomores, and freshmen, shaking her head, page after page. "That's okay," Miss Ames said, and closed the book. We were quiet for a while and sat doodling in our notebooks.

"What I hate is the thought that we're just waiting for something else to happen," I said.

"Well, at least we're giving them a place to sound off. We published this faction's letter. Maybe they'll write again, give us some clues. Maybe that will be enough," Miss Ames said. "We're all waiting. The principal is taking this very seriously."

• • •

Things were piling up on me. I had a difficult paper to write for my AP English class on how Ernest Hemingway's style relates to the main character's detachment in the novel we just read. I had to go over a catalog at the Melody Inn and help select Christmas items to sell in the Gift Shoppe. I needed to help Sylvia get the house ready for Thanksgiving. I still had not written the feature article I'd promised myself I would do back in September in memory of Mark Stedmeister. And I had to finish Part II of the application to the U of Maryland, not to mention full applications to the University of North Carolina at Chapel Hill and William and Mary. Just the list of stuff I had to enclose for Maryland was nerve-wracking: SAT scores; a 500-word essay; a response to each of the questions on page 11 of the application, each response five to seven sentences long; a résumé listing all of my experiences, interests, and extracurricular activities; a description of one activity most enjoyed by me and why. . . .

I scanned the list of questions: *If you could invent one useful thing for humankind, what would it be? Does multidisciplinary teamwork with a faculty mentor, lasting throughout your undergraduate years and dealing with the social implications of science and technology, appeal to you?* Huh? *How has your life experience and background shaped you into an individual who will enrich the University of Maryland community?*

Usually Dad took a cup of coffee with him into the family room and turned on the news after dinner if it wasn't his night to clean up the kitchen. But lately he'd been doing neither. He'd bring a folder of sales figures home from the store and go over his inventory, salaries, bills, rent. . . . Melody Inn headquarters had announced the closing of three stores on the East Coast. Ours wasn't one of them, but what if there were more?

In the past I would have curled up beside him on the couch and gone over some of the questions on the application—testing my answers out on him, how they might affect my admission. But now, more than ever, I realized I was supposed to be figuring all this out on my own. Even if I chose Maryland and lived at home to save Dad the cost of room and board, I would be expected to do the work myself. What if I gave up my chance to go to another school, another state, only to find that I wouldn't have the reassurance and support I'd wanted here at home?

From my chair at the dining room table, where I was drafting my responses to the application, I watched Sylvia sitting across from Dad, her chin in one hand, brows furrowed.

"It doesn't seem possible," I heard Dad say.

"Last year at this time, sales were up thirteen percent."

"Maybe people haven't started Christmas shopping in earnest," Sylvia said. "Things will probably pick up once Thanksgiving's over."

Dad took off his glasses and rubbed his eyes. "The shoe store down the street went out of business today."

"Lawfords? Really?"

"Yeah."

Sylvia sighed. "That's not good, is it? But the restaurant beside you is doing okay. That's always a draw for customers."

"It'll be tight this year, Sylvia. Really tight."

"I know."

"No trips to New York, I'm afraid. No New England tour in the fall. . . ."

"We can make it, Ben. I can live without a weekend of theater-hopping. And those trees in Vermont will still be there next year and the next."

I returned to my application to U of Maryland.

There were other things to concentrate on, though: Thanksgiving, the Snow Ball, Patrick, Christmas. . . .

Gwen had an idea for the Snow Ball, one of the two formal dances at our school. I could tell by her expression that it was going to be something different.

"Let's all trade dresses."

The four of us had gone to the mall Thursday night to hunt for dresses. Shop after shop, we looked the merchandise over and said, "Blah." Nothing looked that great—great enough to spend a hundred and fifty bucks on, anyway. We were standing outside of Macy's and turned to stare at her.

"You're serious?" I said.

"Yeah. It's crazy to buy new dresses right now, and when are we going to wear formal gowns once we get to college? From then on, it'll be bridesmaid dresses, right? No bride is going to want her attendants in leftover Snow Ball dresses."

"But we're not all the same size!" said Liz.

"Pamela and I are about the same, and so are you and Alice."

Smiles traveled from one of us to the other, and then they turned into grins.

"Let's do it!" said Liz, and we all high-fived each other and began chattering at once—colors, shoes, straps or strapless. . . .

And then I added a P.S. to Gwen's suggestion: We would announce it in advance. In fact, I'd get Sam to take a picture of all four of us and put it on the front page of *The Edge*—the very next issue, if we could get our act together in time. LATEST FASHION: DRESS EXCHANGE, could be the heading, and we'd lead off the story with, *Senior girls start new trend. . . .*

I'm sure we sounded like a bunch of chickens as we rode down the escalator and took over one of the tables by the ice-cream shop.

"Okay," said Liz. "What have we got?"

"Last year I wore that slinky black halter-top," I said.

"I loved that dress!" said Liz. "Oh, I can't wait." Then she hesitated. "I've just got that rose-colored crepe. . . ."

We both winced. Not with my strawberry blond hair, and not crepe.

"What did you wear last to the Jack of Hearts dance, Gwen?" Liz asked.

"The Kelly green number with the tiny black polka dots, remember? I'll bet you could wear it, Alice, because it was little big for me."

"With the wide black sash at the waist?" I asked. "That was cute."

"That's the one," said Gwen. "And I want to wear Pamela's salmon satin gown with the spaghetti straps."

"You've got it," said Pamela. "But then what will I wear?"

"Remember that midnight blue dress with the iridescent stripes in the skirt that I wore for the

Jack of Hearts dance? Sylvia could alter it for you, I'll bet," I told her.

"I'm up for anything," said Pamela. "Bring on the photographer!"

The following day Les had good news.

"Signed, sealed, and delivered!" he announced when he stopped by for dinner. "My thesis has been accepted, and I graduate December eighteenth, free and clear!"

"Hey, bro!" I said.

"Congratulations, Les!" said Dad, giving him a hug with a couple of back pats thrown in. "What a relief, huh?"

"You're telling me! Had my first good sleep in months."

"Can I help send out the invitations?" asked Sylvia.

"Oh, wow. Invitations! Hadn't even thought about it. Sure!" said Les. "I might even get around to polishing a pair of shoes for the occasion."

Dad said we owed it to Aunt Sally and Uncle Milt to call them, so we sat around the dining room table after we'd enjoyed Sylvia's impromptu dinner of shrimp scampi and a frozen Sara Lee cake, and made the call.

We all knew the routine and were smiling even before the conversation began: Uncle Milt usually answered the phone. We could fill in his part of the conversation just by listening to Les:

"Hi, Milt. How are things? . . . Well, that's why I'm calling. Wanted you and Aunt Sally to be the first to know that my thesis has been accepted and I'm cleared for takeoff." Les was grinning. "Me too. . . . Yeah, it's been a long road, that's for sure. . . . Roger that. . . . Uh-huh. Seems like I've been in school forever. . . ."

At some point, we knew, the phone would be handed over to Aunt Sally.

"Sure," Les was saying, "put her on. . . . Hi, Sal! Yes. . . . Yes. . . . Well, thank you. I appreciate it. . . . Yeah, I wish Mom were here too. . . . I understand. . . . Of course. . . ."

They were so proud. . . . Mom would be so proud of him. . . . They might not be able to make the ceremony. . . .

And then Les said, "Certainly! I'll put her on," and handed the phone to me. "Aunt Sally wants a word with Alice," he said, sotto voce to Dad and Sylvia, his eyes filled with amusement.

Me? I mouthed, shaking my head. When Aunt Sally, bless her bones, wants to talk to me, it's always an admonition of some kind. It fell to her to help raise us after Mom died, and she's still trying to do her best.

I rolled my eyes and took the phone while the others smiled and settled back, picking at the last crumbs of chocolate cake.

"Hi, Aunt Sally," I said. "It's wonderful news, isn't it?"

"It certainly is" came my aunt's voice, and either my hearing is so acute or her voice is so loud that I always have to hold the phone an inch away from my ear. "With everything going on in the world, it's nice to know that somebody's got it right. Oh, Alice, Marie would be so thrilled. Whoever thought that *Lester* . . . ?" She paused, and I saw Lester's eyes open wide in amusement.

"You never thought he'd make it?" I asked, making a face at Les.

"I just . . . wasn't sure. He always seemed to march to a different drummer, that boy! That band he had once? You know, the Naked Savages—"

"Nomads," I said. "Naked Nomads."

"And all those girlfriends?"

Sylvia had her head on her arms, and her shoulders were shaking with laughter. I had to struggle to keep from laughing too.

"Well, I just don't know," Aunt Sally went on. "But I remember saying to Milt somewhere along the line, 'It's a good thing they left Chicago when they did and moved to Maryland, because if they'd stayed here, Lester might have ended up in that mansion with all those rabbits.'"

Dad and Lester stared at each other, and then they broke out in silent laughter, but I didn't know what they were talking about.

"Rabbits?"

Aunt Sally cleared her throat. "You know . . . that Hefner man . . . and his little playmates."

I looked helplessly at Dad and Lester.

"Hugh Hefner and his Playboy bunnies," Dad whispered. "The Playboy Mansion."

"Oh!" I said to Aunt Sally. "Hugh Hefner and the Playboy Mansion. Why, Aunt Sally, if I'd known it was in Chicago, I'd have toured it while I was there for Carol's wedding."

Aunt Sally gasped.

"Joke! Joke!" I said, trying to remember that we were sharing good news here.

"But this is what I wanted to say to you, Alice," Aunt Sally continued, lowering her voice, conscious, perhaps, that the others could hear. "The newspapers are full of stories about young men who get to the pinnacle of their success and suddenly they self-destruct."

"They do?" I said.

"They do! You read about it all the time. A football player dies of an overdose; a politician gets drunk and kills someone with his car; a movie star leaves his wife and children. . . ."

"I don't know, Aunt Sally," I said. "Les isn't married, he's not running for office, and he doesn't play football."

The family stared at me, then covered their mouths and laughed some more.

"I just want you to keep an eye on him for me," Aunt Sally said. "With the economy the way it is and people losing their jobs, I didn't want to worry Ben or Sylvia, but do give Lester special attention right now, will you? Make sure he eats well and gets plenty of sleep and doesn't get so full of himself that he thinks he's above the law."

"I'll watch him every spare minute I get," I told her. "He just wanted you to know the good news. Pass it along to Carol and Larry for us. How are things with them?"

"Well, they haven't given me a grandchild yet."

"They just got married in July!" I spluttered.

This time Aunt Sally laughed at her own joke. "Of course. And they're happy."

We were too when the conversation ended at last.

"Okay, spill it," said Les when I'd hung up and we erupted in laughter. "What's she worried about now?"

"That you'll self-destruct," I told him. "You'll drive too fast, eat too much, sleep too little, and end up in the Playboy Mansion with all those bunnies."

Dad was laughing so hard, he had to pull out his handkerchief and wipe his eyes. "What would we ever do without old Sal?" he said. "Every family should have one, I guess, but ours is the genuine article."

14

Relationships

Big news flash. For our crowd, anyway. Something gossipy and trite in the general scheme of things, but a fact we could chew on awhile to forget the Nazi stuff at school and all the anxiety over college: Jill and Justin broke up.

Pamela and I were trying to figure out just how long they'd been a couple.

"I know they started going out the summer before tenth grade," Pamela said, passing around the bag of Fritos Gwen had brought. Pam had invited the three of us to sleep over on Saturday. Mr. Jones and Meredith, his fiancée, had gone to a movie.

"I think it might even have been before then. By that summer they were sleeping with each other," Liz said, and added comically, "I was shocked, I tell you! *Shocked!*"

We laughed.

"They probably had one of the longest

relationships of any couple in school," said Gwen. "I'll give them that. But Justin—I think he deserves better than Jill, if you want my opinion."

"I think he deserves just what he got," I put in, remembering that he used to like Liz, and I'd hoped maybe those two would click. "Still, guys don't think a whole lot about relationships when they're freshmen. Sophomores, even."

"And who really knows what goes on between two people?" said Gwen.

"We do," said Pamela, grinning. "Jill loved to tell us every little detail. She'd tell you exactly what went on between the sheets if you asked her. And the answer was 'Plenty.'"

"So which of them called it off?" asked Liz.

"Jill," said Pamela. "I got it straight from Karen, and if Karen doesn't know, nobody does. Jill's furious at the way the Colliers have tried to break them up. She and Justin's mom in particular hate each other, and I guess she gave Justin an ultimatum: Stand up to your mom or else."

We groaned.

"Ohhh, bad call!" I said. "What did she expect him to do? Pack up his bags and say, 'Well, Mom, I'm outta here?' Is Jill nuts? Where would he go? Who foots the bill for college next year?"

"Jill's used to getting her way, that's all," said Pamela. "But his parents think she's after their money."

"And isn't she?" asked Liz.

"I don't know. But I think that when a couple's been together as long as they have, there's got to be a little something more," Pamela answered. "Jill's gorgeous—you've got to hand her that. There are a dozen guys who would love to go out with her."

We ambled out to the kitchen to see what Meredith had left for our dinner, and Pamela slung plates onto the table like she was dealing cards.

"How did the Colliers get so rich?" I asked. "I thought his dad was in the navy. You don't get rich in the navy."

"*Was,*" said Pamela. "Career officer, but he retired and became a partner in his dad's real estate firm. You know, Collier and Sons? You see their signs everywhere. It was his grandfather, I think, who really had the dough."

"So how is Justin taking the breakup?" asked Gwen.

"Awful, according to Karen. Keeps calling Jill's number and she won't answer."

"Time for Mommy and Daddy to whisk him off to the Bahamas again," I said. "Remember how they did that on spring break last year, just to get him away from Jill, and Justin sent her money for a plane ticket and put her up in the hotel next door?"

We all whooped at the memory as we waited for the meat loaf and potatoes to heat up in the microwave. Gwen passed the silverware around.

"Speaking of couples," said Liz, "when are your dad and Meredith going to tie the knot, Pam?"

"Who knows?" said Pamela.

I wondered if I could ask the question the rest of us were thinking. "Is it possible he's still . . . well . . . that your mom's still on his radar?"

"Veto that," said Pamela. "She's dating someone from Nordstrom, and they're hitting it off. A nice man, let me add—a manager from another store. No, my guess is that Dad and Meredith are waiting for me to graduate and go off to school somewhere so they can start married life in the house all to themselves. I can't blame them for that."

Sitting across from her, I slowly sipped my glass of iced tea, wondering if Dad and Sylvia have been waiting for *me* to clear out so that at last *they* can have the place to themselves.

At school even Daniel had heard about the "breakup of the year."

"How do you do a breakup?" he asked me as we sat in the library during lunch when I'd volunteered to help him with an assignment.

"It's not anything formal," I explained. "Either the girl or the guy tells the other it's over."

"Nothing is broken? Smashed?"

"No. There's no ritual. It just means the

relationship is through. That they can each start going out with other people."

Daniel leaned back in his chair, deep in thought, skinny arms folded over his chest, chin tucked down. "That is hard to do in America for my brother. He would like some day to find a bride, but your ways and the Dinka ways are different."

"Your culture? What would be the Dinka way for a man to find a wife?" I asked.

"I remember once, before we left our village, when the young men would gather. They would stand and sing for the girls and laugh. And the girls would smile at them. And they danced. I was only a small boy, but I liked to see the dancing."

"And that's where a man would meet his bride?"

"Perhaps a man and a girl would make plans to meet again. A man would go a long way off to visit a girl from another village. Even if the weather was very bad, a man would go. The more bad the weather, the more—how do you say?— more impress the woman would be. But . . ."

He sighed and slid down a little farther in his chair. "A man wanting a bride would have cattle. And that would be the dowry. In a refugee camp no man had cattle. All he had for a dowry was a promise."

"Is your brother looking for a bride here?" I asked.

Daniel shook his head. "Geri looks only at his

books. He says first he goes to school. Then he finds a bride. I think he will find a bride in Africa, but he is like all men. He will want a wife."

Daniel looked at me then and laughed, a somewhat silly laugh. I could never quite tell if he found something amusing or if he was merely feeling self-conscious.

"What is your family doing for Thanksgiving?" I asked him. The week before, he had been asking Phil about American holidays, and Phil had given him a calendar with the days marked.

"Our mother will be cooking in the restaurant where she helps out. She will go in very early and come home very late," he said.

"Then why don't you and your brother come to our house for dinner?" I asked, sure it would be all right with Dad and Sylvia.

"We will come!" Daniel said enthusiastically. "We will bring a roasted pig."

"What?"

This time Daniel broke into full laughter, getting the attention of students at the other tables. He ducked down again, still grinning. "No pig," he said.

I got Sam to come over on Monday night with his camera and take a picture of Gwen, Pamela, Liz, and me in our traded dresses. We didn't do our hair or makeup.

"If everybody knows in advance what we'll be wearing, we've at least got to keep *something* a surprise," said Pamela.

It was a riot. Gwen's green and black polka dot dress was too tight for me, so I left the zipper open in back beneath the wide sash. My midnight blue dress was way too big in the torso for Pamela, so for the picture—the four of us lined up with our arms around each other—Gwen and I had a hand in back and each of us tightly clasped a big hunk of material to make Pamela's dress look, from the front, like it fit. Gwen was really hot in Pamela's salmon-colored dress with the spaghetti straps, and Liz looked seductive in my black halter dress.

"Say cheese," said Sam. "Woops. No, wait a minute. Gwen, that neckline is really dipping on the left."

We glanced over and saw half a breast visible— she needed a strapless bra and hadn't brought one, so she wasn't wearing any. We howled as Sylvia moved in with a box of pins and pulled the strap down some in back.

Sam said he got at least three good pictures, and we could come by the newspaper office the following day when he'd have them at full size, so we could choose the one we liked best.

After he left, Pamela said, "Now all we need for the Snow Ball are dates. You going with Keeno, Liz?"

"Yeah, I mentioned it to him," Liz said.

"*Mentioned* it? Are you guys in a relationship or not?"

"We don't label it. We're just really close."

"Alice is going with Daniel, I'm going with Austin, Liz is going with Keeno, what about you, Pamela?" Gwen asked.

"Why don't you ask Louie and we'll double," said Liz.

"Keeno's friend from St. John's?" said Pamela. "I hardly even know him."

"So what? You've seen each other naked— how much more do you have to know?" Gwen joked.

"Shhhh," I said as Sylvia gave us a wary smile and raised one eyebrow. "Erase, erase. Why don't we all go together? Invite Louie, Pamela, and we'll make it eight."

"Okay," said Pamela. "Dress? Check. Date? Check. This'll be the easiest dance I ever attended. I'll worry about shoes later."

Sylvia went over our dresses while we were still wearing them, pinning up sides here and there and marking what needed to be let out.

"I'm not a fancy seamstress, girls, but I don't think anyone will notice my alterations," she promised. "There's just one problem," she added with a twinkle in her eye. "The dresses self-destruct if you try to take them off."

• • •

The photo looked great on the front page of the school newspaper, and Phil liked my idea and headline. *Four senior girls*, the article began, *have caught the wave of a new trend for school dances: exchanging dresses with each other.* This, of course, made it seem as though it must be happening all over the country, but so much the better.

Though we had one of the other reporters write this particular story, it was a thrill to see my byline under a growing number of feature articles—one on our new football coach and his family and, in this issue, one on relationships.

I hadn't even imagined that Jill and Justin were going to break up when I wrote the relationship piece; it was a follow-up to a question the roving reporters had asked in a recent survey:

HOW DO YOU DEFINE A
"RELATIONSHIP"?

I'd say exclusive dating a few
months or more.
                    —Marcella Bogdan, senior

Why do you have to call it
anything? Why can't it just be
"guy likes girl," "girl likes guy"?
                    —Chris Weil, junior

You've got to at least know her last
name.

—Jim Donovitch, senior

I'd picked up on that second comment for my
article—that from what I'd gathered, listening
to people talk, girls were usually the ones who
wanted it defined:

> The big question for girls is "Are
> we going together or not?" And if
> the guy agrees that "Yeah, we're
> going out," the girl wants a name
> for it. "Are we a couple? Is this a
> relationship or just a hookup?"

Amy had heard a lot of talk about Jill and
Justin too, and when I told her that it was sort of
awkward, my feature article coming out practically
the very week the breakup had happened, Amy
wanted to know who broke it off, Jill or Justin.

"I heard it was Jill," I said.

She was mystified. "If I had a boyfriend, I'd
keep him," she said.

"Well, some time you will, Amy," I told her.
"By the way, you've been looking great these days."

She really was looking better, dressing more
carefully, choosing more figure-fitting clothes.

"I did my nails," she said proudly, and held

out her hands. The nails were bright pink, with a little rose stenciled on the ring finger of both hands.

"They look fantastic, and you've been doing a super job as a roving reporter," I said.

"I like asking questions," she said. "It used to be when kids saw me coming, they'd whisper and turn away. Now you know what a boy said?"

"What?"

"He said, 'You want to ask me a question, Amy?' And I said, 'Yes. How do you define a relationship?' and he said, 'The first time a girl asks me out, I'll call it a relationship.' And then he said, 'No, don't put that in the newspaper. I was just kidding.' And I said I wouldn't. But he was nice."

"That was a good decision," I said. "If a person asks for a remark to be off the record, you have to respect that."

"Off the record," Amy said, and she fumbled around with her notebook and wrote it down.

It did seem to me that Amy was happier, but she also seemed a little more excitable and flustered than usual. There was just a certain charm about her in the brave and hungry way she approached life, and I figured if I accomplished nothing more my senior year, I'd at least done well by helping her become a roving reporter. The truth was I loved my job as features editor.

I felt needed, appreciated, and capable when I was in the newsroom, and I even wondered now and then if I should major in journalism instead of counseling when I got to college.

We hadn't heard the last of Bob White. Hadn't expected to, actually. This time, though, the note was typed on a computer, and it was even more hateful than the one before. It was also unsigned:

> The only way to save this country
> is to take back our streets and our
> schools and kick ass. If we let the
> Jews, the beaners, and the black
> vermin take over, who's going to
> carry the torch for the white race?

We silently passed the note around the conference table.

"This doesn't even sound like the same person," said Phil. "I don't think it is."

Tim nodded. "We're dealing with more than one. They know we're not going to print this, though, so what's the point?"

"To let us know they haven't backed off. That they're still out there," said Phil.

And that was the chilling part. *They're out there.*

15

Dinner Guests

Sylvia and I set a beautiful table on Thanksgiving. Some of the decorations she had brought along after she married Dad were two little log cabins, the kind the Pilgrims might have built, that were also candleholders. We put them at each end of the table, with a low bouquet of carnations in fall colors in between.

I'd baked two pies the night before—pumpkin and pecan—and Dad was doing the turkey. Sylvia took over the mashed potatoes and veggies; Les and Paul, his roommate, were bringing wine; and Kay, whom Dad had invited at the last minute because her parents were out of the country, was bringing a salad. We hadn't expected anything of Daniel and his brother, of course. I figured it would be culture shock enough just eating at a table with Lester.

Daniel and Geri arrived first. "We are on time!" Daniel announced proudly.

"We Sudanese are notoriously late for

appointments in our own country, but in the United States of America we do as Americans do," said his brother. "I am Geri."

"Welcome!" Sylvia said. "Some of us are notoriously late for appointments too. Please come in. I'm Sylvia."

Geri was just as thin as his brother, cheekbones prominent like Daniel's, his skin even darker, but he was taller by four inches. Both of them wore lighter jackets than seemed practical for November.

Geri handed Sylvia a baking pan covered with foil. "This is a gift from our mother for your table. It is a special dish that we enjoy very much in Sudan."

"Well, we're glad to have you. Oh, it smells delicious! Thank you so much," Sylvia said, and introduced Dad, who came in from the kitchen.

"Come on back to the next room," Dad coaxed. "We've got a good fire going." They seemed reluctant to let go of their jackets so Dad let them keep them on. But they had barely sat down before the doorbell rang again, and this time it was Kay, with a large salad bowl in her arms, a bottle of dressing in one hand.

"Did you know it's snowing?" she asked. "Hi, Mr. M. Hi, Sylvia." Dad took her coat, but at the word *snow*, both Daniel and his brother went hurrying to the windows in the family room.

We had to look hard to see the flakes, but they were in the air, melting the minute they hit the ground. Daniel was entranced, though not enough to go back out in the cold.

"When do you make the men?" he asked.

"The *snow*men?" I guessed. "It has to come down a lot harder than this." I introduced Kay to them just as we heard Les and Paul arriving, and suddenly the house was filled with voices and introductions and exclamations about the possibility for a white Christmas.

There were the usual murmurs of praise as each person was asked to pass the platter closest to him. Geri asked about each dish and its relationship to Thanksgiving, and Sylvia gave a brief synopsis of the first somewhat mythical Thanksgiving Day.

Les, knowing he had a captive audience, couldn't help adding his own version: "With only two drumsticks per turkey, of course, the early colonists were already figuring out how they could trade each drumstick for a river valley, while the wily Indians offered a few steaming ears of corn for all the pies on the table."

"Les!" I said. "It's going to take me a week to untangle all that for Daniel. Why don't you say something useful?"

Lester pondered that a moment. "Hmm.

Useful," he said. "Okay. How's this?" He held out his plate for Daniel and Geri to see, pointing to the turkey and mashed potatoes. "The bland and the bland," he said. He added a scoopful of dressing to the plate. "The *pièce de résistance*," he intoned, and then, lifting the ladle from the gravy boat, "and this is the gold that binds it all together." He poured the gravy over the meat, potatoes, and dressing, and in a final flourish, he added a little spoonful of cranberry sauce atop the heap.

Daniel and Geri, glad for the demonstration, prepared their own plates in the same manner, interrupted now and then with the arrival of hot rolls and sweet potatoes and green bean casserole.

"Whatever this is, it's delicious!" Kay said, savoring a mouthful of the dish Geri and Daniel had brought. She dissected another spoonful on her plate. "Spinach . . . peanuts? . . . some kind of wonderful spice . . ."

"It's my favorite," said Daniel. "Our mother cooks this for the restaurant where she works, in exchange for our apartment."

"How does that work?" Kay asked him.

"I am here because of a scholarship to George Washington University," Geri explained. "A church sponsored our mother and Daniel, and we live in an apartment owned by a man in the church who also owns a restaurant. That's where our mother is today—cooking."

"My parents are on a cruise, or I'd be at their place," said Paul.

"Mine are visiting family in China, or I would be eating with them," said Kay. "This is so wonderful, Mr. M—inviting me here."

"Then you, too, are a long way from home," Geri told her.

"Not really," said Kay, pushing back the shiny lock of hair that kept falling over one eye. "I was born in China, but this has always seemed like home to me. We've been back twice, both times before I was ten, but I don't remember a lot. I didn't want to go with them this time because I need to work; I'm saving for grad school."

"I would like to go back to Sudan as a lawyer," Geri told us. "I will be going back whether I work in law or not—that is the agreement. But I hope to be able to help my people make a better government."

I noticed that Daniel was paying close attention to how we ate—what we ate with our fingers and when we used a fork or knife. By the time the platters were passed around the second time, however, he didn't seem to care. He and his brother loved the meat, and they had second and third helpings.

When there was a pause in the conversation, I asked Les how George and Joan's wedding had gone.

"I didn't tell you?" Les said. Then he filled in the rest of the table: "George Palamas was our former roommate, and it was almost the wedding-that-wasn't."

"He tried to back out?" I asked.

"No. Sprained an ankle. The morning of the wedding, he was running up our side steps with his tux and tripped over the bottom of the dry-cleaning bag. We got an Ace bandage and bound him up as best we could, gave him a couple ibuprofen, and he held out long enough to dance with his bride at the reception. Then they were off to Greece for the honeymoon, and I haven't heard from him since."

"That's awful, spraining his ankle!" Sylvia said.

"Yeah. I was the best man," said Paul. "I could see sweat on his brow. I slipped him another pill when I gave him the ring, and I think he swallowed it without water just before they came back up the aisle."

"Well, better his ankle than getting cold feet," I said.

Daniel looked from Paul to me. "A man with cold feet cannot marry?"

We all broke into laughter.

"It's an expression, Daniel," I said. "It means he's having second thoughts." And when I still wasn't making myself clear, I said, "When a man or woman doesn't want to marry after all."

Geri shook his head. "That would not be good."

"What are weddings like in your country?" Dad asked.

"There were no big weddings in the refugee camp, and we were there since I was nine," Geri said. "But I remember some when we were still in the south. Those were great times and would last for several days. The bridal dance would go on almost till morning, with much singing. Now the wedding party must end before sunset prayers and be supervised by sheiks and the police. It is not a happy time for Sudan."

"Are the marriages arranged?" asked Kay, who was helping Sylvia pass slices of pie around the table, followed by a bowl of whipped cream.

"It is the joining of two families, and all are concerned with the arrangements, but there must be approval by the spouses," Geri explained.

"My parents had an arranged marriage, and it seems to have worked for them," Kay told us. "They're modern in some ways but old country in others. They want me to meet a son of their Chinese friends. I know that's why they wanted me to come with them this time."

"Maybe you'd end up liking the guy," I suggested.

Kay gave me an anguished look. "I already have a boyfriend, and he's not Asian. I met him my senior year at Georgetown, and I don't know how to tell my parents. They don't even know I'm seeing anyone. They think I only go out with girlfriends. I would be with my boyfriend today, but he's a part-time waiter at the Hyatt and had to work."

"Perhaps your parents would like him if they met him," Sylvia suggested.

Kay shook her head. "No, I'm afraid not. They didn't let me date all through high school. 'Concentrate on your studies,' they would say. 'A boyfriend will not help you get to college.' Well, I got through college, and you'd think I could make some decisions myself, but they say, 'Trust us, we know best.' When you're an only child, so much is expected of you. They sacrifice so you can go to school, so you can go to college, have the best tutors, the music lessons, the chess, the challenges. . . . And then, when you disappoint them . . ."

"This all must be very hard on you," Sylvia sympathized.

"It's hard in one way, easy in another. When you have your life all laid out for you—what school to attend, what courses to study, how long you study, where you live, whom you marry— you don't have to worry about choices," Kay said. "You don't have to decide between this or that. It's all arranged for you. But it's hard because I might find—when I'm forty—that it's someone else's life I'm living . . . my parents', not my own."

There were a few seconds of silence while we thought that one over. Then Les raised his wineglass and said genially, "To life, everybody, confusing as it is!"

"To life!" we said, clinking our glasses, and I know we were all thinking about how lucky—or unlucky—we were.

On Saturday we had a girls' night out. Molly Brennan was home for the weekend from the U of Maryland, still leukemia-free, and Gwen brought her friend Yolanda. We went to a chick flick, and Yolanda said we could celebrate the loss of her V card. Gwen said maybe we should just celebrate Thanksgiving break.

The guys would have hated the movie—all about weddings and mix-ups and breakups and makeups, and so Hollywood that you could almost predict exactly where the car chase would take place and about when Mr. Right would enter the picture. It was afterward that we had the best time—at a little Greek restaurant where you could spend a couple hours just drinking strong coffee and eating appetizers. I told them about Kay's American boyfriend.

"I can't believe her parents are still so controlling when she's out of college!" I said. "I mean,

I understand we're from different cultures, but why do they assume she'd be happier with an Asian boyfriend? She hardly even remembers China. She lives here now."

"Birds of a feather . . . ," said Pamela.

"Like that kook's letters in *The Edge* about keeping the races separate and pure," said Liz.

Gwen reached across the table and helped herself to the pita bread I'd left on my plate. "I don't know. Whether we like to admit it or not, we *do* like to be with 'our own kind' sometimes."

"Never thought you'd say that," Pamela said. "I'd think you'd be sick to death of people saying they're happier 'with their own kind.'"

"It's the 'sometimes' that's important," put in Yolanda, caressing one of her dangly earrings. Her nails, half an inch long, were painted a bright canary yellow.

"Let's face it," Gwen went on, "there are things African Americans share that you just don't, that's all. Like, my grandmother can tell you about driving through the South and going straight through certain towns, no matter how hungry you were, because it just wasn't safe to stop. And when you did finally find a place to eat—even a take-out joint—you had to go around to the back door and pay for your supper there. Eat it back by the trash cans or in your car."

We had no answer for that.

"Yeah, and sometimes when I get together with my cousins," added Yolanda, "especially with Aunt Josie, we get to laughing and talking black English, and you wouldn't understand a word we were saying. Just something fun to do. We can talk about straightening hair, we can sway when we sing in church—stuff that may not have any meaning to you. Maybe Kay's parents feel the same about wanting her to marry an Asian."

"But . . . if you carry this out to its logical conclusion . . . ," I protested.

"No, you don't carry it out to any conclusion. You don't make it more than it is," said Molly, siding with Gwen. "Just because we're having a girls' night out, does it mean we don't want to get together with guys?"

"No!" we all chorused.

Molly was looking especially good in a cobalt blue sweater that made her wide blue eyes all the brighter, and she had a new haircut—loose curls about the face. It had grown out now a couple inches. "And by the way," she added, "I've got a boyfriend."

We pounded the table and cheered. Molly, one of our favorite people, who once told us she'd never been kissed. "Tell! Tell!" we begged.

"Well, he's Indian. Pakistani, anyway. And my folks love him."

We hugged Molly and gushed some more.

"And is he a good kisser?" Pamela asked her.

"You'd better believe it," said Molly mischievously. "I'm making up for lost time."

16

Amy

Because we'd had only three days of school the week before Thanksgiving, we'd delayed the printing of *The Edge* until this week. We still had a couple of things to add. One of the roving reporters had done a short piece on consignment shops catering to teens, where girls could get long dresses and heels and beaded clutch bags at fantastic prices. I had to edit it a little, but we wanted to make sure the story got in this issue, with only one full weekend left before the Snow Ball. And because Amy had done some of the calling to the consignment shops to get their contact info, her name was included in the byline. She was thrilled.

I stayed after school on Monday to research white supremacy groups, but all I really had to do was Google the term *hate groups* and I was in. So many different names! So many disguises! I'd read that what you first see on the Internet is fairly benign: *Our goal is simple—to show white youth a better way of life and teach them a sense of racial awareness and pride.*

Then you dig a little deeper and you get, *Bring our troops home and put them on the Mexican border* or, *Money given to a church may end up going to help irresponsible people who live just like parasites on the goodwill of society.* I even found a site promoting some kind of racial test. It said, *If the results show that you have a moderate or extreme bias in favor of whites, you are okay. If you get any other result, you could be at greater risk of being cheated, robbed, raped, or even murdered. . . .* Implying, of course, that if you choose mostly white, Protestant Anglo-Saxons as friends, you can live a relatively safe life. But if you start hanging around with Jews, you're at risk of being cheated; with Hispanics, of being robbed; with African Americans, of being raped or murdered.

There were promotions for musical and rap groups spewing out hate; preachers, black and white, predicting war between the races. Looking forward to it, actually. Our library received a magazine called *Intelligence Report* that kept tabs on hate groups, their leaders and methods, all over the United States. When Phil joined me at a table, we leafed through back issues, studying the ways the groups operate: racist disc jockeys with a new brand of neo-Nazi music; Holocaust deniers claiming that the German concentration camps during World War II were really filled with criminals or typhus victims; Klu Klux Klan supporters advocating death to the president.

Phil showed me a photo of a young woman wearing an American flag as a sarong, her face contorted with contempt, holding up a sign reading GOD HATES FAGS. Another of young children giving the Heil Hitler salute. "It just keeps coming," I said. "All the hate."

"So . . . we'll keep writing about it," he said. "We'll come at it from different angles. Think we should devote a whole issue to it?"

I thought about it a moment. "Let me see how much of this stuff I can stomach at one time," I told him.

Pamela called me that night. "About this dress exchange . . . ," she said.

"Yeah?"

"Can we exchange guys, too?"

"You want to swap *dates*?"

"I called Louie to invite him, and he said okay . . . and then he *belched*."

"Whoa!" I said. "You mean that was part of the response?"

"I don't know. He excused himself, of course. He said he'd just had dinner, but still. . . ."

"Was the burp a part of the 'okay,' or was

it 'okay' and then a silence and *then* a burp?" I asked her. I saw Dad staring at me from across the room.

"Sort of part of the 'okay,' I guess," said Pamela.

"Was that the whole conversation?"

"No. He asked about flowers and who we were going with and the color of my dress and everything, but I think . . . I *thought* . . . I heard another belch toward the end. I mean, I was going to ask him what he'd had for dinner, but then I figured I wasn't supposed to have heard it. But if we're dancing and he's belching—"

"Pamela, this is the first guy you've gone out with since you and Tim broke up. Right?"

"Yeah."

"And Tim never belched the whole time you were with him?"

"I can't say that."

"He never grunted or scratched or blew his nose or picked his teeth? Never?"

"He probably did, but not on our first date."

"Pamela, chill," I told her. "You are going to the dance with Louie. Now cut him a little slack, huh? For all you know, your stomach is going to growl during a slow number."

"Now I have something new to worry about."

"Good. If your stomach growls, it cancels out his burp. Period," I said.

When I hung up, Dad was still staring at me.

I started to explain, but he said, "I don't even want to know," and he settled down again with the paper.

After school on Tuesday, I stayed late again to check in with our counselor, Mrs. Bailey, about my college applications. By the time I left her office, it was twenty of five. I was walking down the hall toward my locker when I saw Dennis Granger come out of his classroom farther on, pulling on his jacket and heading toward the south exit. I automatically slowed, not wanting to let him hear my footsteps and be in an empty corridor with the man after school hours.

I wondered about the teacher he was subbing for this year—if she had had her baby yet and whether she was even coming back. How you manage motherhood and a career. Wondered if I should do a feature article on substitute teachers and what it's like to suddenly take on a class for a semester when you don't know the students, possibly not even the subject, and have nothing to go on except the teacher's class notes for the course.

No, I decided. It could undermine substitute teachers' influence on a class to find out just how unprepared, and possibly nervous, some of them were. And I sure wasn't about to interview Dennis Granger. I waited until I saw him disappear down the steps at the end of the hall, and then I walked on.

I was just passing the door of the darkened classroom when I heard someone crying—soft little sobs, like whispered speech. I stopped, listened, and tried to see through the glass. Finally I opened the door.

At first I didn't see anything, as the shades had been drawn against the afternoon sun. Then I noticed a girl leaning against the wall in one corner, hands over her face, her shoulders shaking.

"Amy!" I said, and went quickly over to her. "What happened? Are you okay?" But the sight of her disheveled clothes made me sick to my stomach, and the dark stillness of the room gave it an aura of evil.

Amy's face was turned to one side, as though she couldn't look at me, and she covered the front of her khaki skirt with both hands.

My heart was pounding furiously. I didn't know whether to go screaming after Dennis Granger or stay with her.

"Amy," I said again, gently clasping her arms and looking her over. "You're *not* okay, are you?"

She shook her head, but tried to stop her sobs. "Hi . . . A-A-Alice," she said jerkily, tugging her clothes back in place.

"I saw Mr. Granger leaving," I said. "What happened in here?"

She wouldn't look at me. "He . . . helps . . . me with English," she said finally.

I backed off and stared at her. "*Granger's* your tutor? You've been coming to *him*?" *Oh, God!* "But something else happened, didn't it?" I asked, looking her over carefully. I gently removed the hands that were trying to hide a wet spot on the front of her crumpled skirt. "Amy, tell me. . . ." And now my own voice was trembling. "Did Mr. Granger rape you?"

"No!" she said explosively.

"Did you have your underwear off?"

"No, Alice. I don't take my underwear off for guys, even when they ask," she said.

"Did . . . did he ask?"

She wouldn't answer.

I felt we had both been violated somehow. That we had both been molested, one way or another, here at school. I wanted to get out of that room, but Amy wasn't ready yet, still crying.

"Please tell me what happened," I begged.

She sniffled some more but began shaking her head again. "I'm not going to come back to Mr. Granger anymore. I can do my English myself," she said, and her hand went back to the front of her skirt.

I eased her down in one of the chairs and took the one next to her. "Listen, Amy, this is molesta-tion. If Dennis Granger put his hands under your clothes or pressed against you or anything like that, you need to report it. He pressed against me too."

She glanced at me quickly, then dropped her eyes again. "Did . . . did you report it?"

"Not yet, but I'm going to."

Amy scrunched up her face so tightly that her eyes closed. She shook her head. "I didn't get raped," she repeated.

"Maybe not, but he took advantage of you— of me—and that's never right for a teacher. For *any* guy. Let's go to the office. I'll go with you."

"*No*, Alice!" she said. "My mom's picking me up at five."

"Then we'll tell your mom."

Amy began crying again. "No! She'll say I did it."

"Did what? No matter what you did, Amy, he's the teacher." I studied her. "Has this happened before?"

"Just . . . well, last week . . . no, the week before . . . when the tutoring was over, I kissed him."

"You . . . kissed him?" It was as though we were suddenly little five-year-old girls searching our way through a forest. Turn here? Turn there? Do this? Do that? At what point was it okay to yell?

"I got a good grade on my English paper,

and it was because he helped me with that part, and I kissed him on the cheek for a thank-you. I've kissed him . . . well, maybe four times when tutoring was over, and . . . well, after the first time he said he liked it so I did it again. My mom would be really mad."

That sick feeling came over me again, and I swallowed. I tried to think of a way to get through to her, but she continued:

"Then . . . last week . . . when I bent over to kiss him, he asked if he could kiss me back, and I said I guessed so, and he got up and put his hands here . . . and here . . . and then he touched me here." She motioned toward her breasts.

"And what happened today, Amy? *I* won't get mad, no matter what." *How skillfully we are manipulated*, I was thinking. *How easy it is not to tell.*

"Well, I didn't kiss him when tutoring was over, because I didn't know if I should. But when we were done, he asked if I was going to kiss him, and I said maybe. He got up and moved me into a corner and kissed me, and this time . . ." She pointed to her breasts again. "He put his hand under my shirt and under my b-b-bra."

Her face was flaming, and she was on the verge of tears again, I could tell. She stopped to take a deep breath. "*Please* don't tell anyone, Alice."

"Amy, whether you kissed him or not, what he did was very wrong, and he knows it. If you don't report this, I will. The principal has to be told."

"No, Alice! Don't! I'll tell . . . I'll tell my dad."

"This is important, Amy! It's serious. Nobody's going to punish you because Mr. Granger knows better. Promise me you'll tell your parents."

She wiped her face and took more deep breaths. "I'll tell," she said, and looked at the clock. "I have to go. Mom will be waiting, and if I'm not there, she says, 'Dawdle, dawdle dilly, that's you.' I hate dawdle dilly."

Amy picked up her book bag and started for the door. I got up too, put my arm around her, and walked along beside her. If I had reported Granger earlier, would this have happened to Amy? But then again, the old doubt: What exactly had he done to me? Who would ever believe it? He'd say that somebody going by had bumped into him, which made him bump into me. Perfectly possible.

"Why are you coming with me?" Amy asked, her voice still a bit breathy.

"Because I know how upset you are. I'm your friend, after all."

"That means you like me, and I like you too," she said.

As we approached the south entrance, I saw

a silver Volvo waiting at the curb. When we got to the door, Amy put out one elbow to block me and said, "I can do this myself."

I hesitated. I had fully intended to walk her to the car, to be there for moral support. But then I realized that I was treating her as though she weren't capable of handling this herself.

"Okay, Amy," I said. "I'll see you tomorrow."

I watched her walk toward the car with her little lopsided gait, drop her bag on the backseat, and climb in the passenger side. I could see a woman's face turned toward Amy, see that something was being asked, something answered, and then . . . in far too short a time, the car moved forward again.

She hadn't told. If she had not told her parents by the time she got to school tomorrow, I would report the incident myself. I wondered if I should go back to Mrs. Bailey and tell her about it right then. But when I got to her office, she had gone.

I worried about Amy all evening. For one thing, if she told her parents what had happened, she would probably mention that she'd talked about it to me, and they might call me to verify her account. In any case, no one called.

But it was equally possible that they would not want to discuss it with anyone other than the principal, or possibly the police, and they could very well show up tomorrow at school. The more I thought about it, though, the more I doubted Amy would tell them. And if she didn't, who should I tell? Her parents? Mrs. Bailey? Mr. Beck?

Twice I was on the verge of talking to Sylvia about it. But the thought of going to her made me feel even more like a child. I'd already lost that assurance of safety and trust you're supposed to get in school. The only way I could see to feel seventeen again was to prove I could handle this myself.

Just thinking about Dennis Granger made me seethe. How did he dare? I didn't have to ask myself what attracted him to Amy. Her vulnerability, her need, her trust. It infuriated me that people like him could masquerade as responsible and caring, all the while trolling for girls like Amy.

I woke twice in the night, wondering if it was time to get up, and finally I rose at five thirty, showered, and was glad when Dad said I could have his car for the day, knowing I had Student Jury after school.

As soon as I got there, I looked for Amy, but I had to turn in some copy at the newsroom and still hadn't seen her when the first bell rang. I began to think she may have stayed home. When I caught sight of Dennis Granger over the lunch hour, chatting it up with students, I knew immediately that he was still on board.

I'll give Amy till two o'clock, I told myself. And then, *I'll give her a half hour more.*

Then I saw her going in a restroom after the last class and followed her in. Another girl was just leaving, and we were alone.

"Amy," I said, "did you tell your parents?"

She didn't answer. She was washing some ink off her hands.

I leaned over so she had to look at me. "Amy, this is too big a thing to keep secret. Not what you did, but what he did. To both of us."

Her lips quivered.

"If we don't report it, he'll go on doing this and embarrassing other girls. He may do more than kissing and touching, and that's not being a good teacher."

"I . . . I know," she said in a small voice.

"Do you want to be a good friend to other girls?"

She looked up at me and nodded seriously.

"Then you'll report this so it won't happen to anyone else. I'll go with you, okay? I'll tell Mr. Beck how Dennis Granger pressed up against me at the drinking fountain, and then it happened to you."

"Okay," she said. "But I wasn't getting a drink of water."

"I know."

Student Jury would be starting soon, but I didn't care. Like soldiers, we marched to the school office and asked for Mr. Beck.

Mrs. Free, his personal secretary, was at Student Jury, so we talked to another woman.

"Mr. Beck's in a meeting right now," she said. "He'll be at least forty minutes."

"It's important!" I said.

"Well, so is this meeting," the secretary said, smiling sympathetically, and added, "School board members."

I tried to think. "Is Mr. Gephardt available?"

"I'm afraid not. He had to leave early."

This cannot be happening! Not after I had to beg and plead to get Amy here.

"Could we make an appointment, then, for Mr. Beck at three thirty? We can't leave until we've seen him," I said. "It's urgent."

I could tell she took me seriously now.

"I'll put you down and ask him not to leave until he's met with you," she said, and took our names.

I looked at the clock. A quarter of three. Student Jury rarely took more than a half hour. Amy and I went out in the hall. She seemed more perky now, more confident. We had an appointment, and I was going with her. Our names were in the book.

"Look, Amy," I said. "I'm going to Student Jury. Why don't you come down to the library. I'll be just across the hall, and as soon as it's over, I'll come and get you. Do you mind waiting in the library?"

"I like to look at *National Geographic*," she said. "Except that I would never take off my clothes for a picture. Mom says they didn't have any clothes on in the first place. I wouldn't want to live in a place you didn't wear clothes."

"How were you going to get home today?" I asked. "I've got Dad's car, so I can drive you. Should you call your mom and tell her you'll be late?"

She pulled her cell phone out of her bag, and we stopped in the hallway to make the call. Amy carefully pressed her index finger on each number, concentrating hard.

"Mom?" she said. "It's Amy. Alice is going to drive me home because we have a meeting." She listened, then looked at me. "What time will we be home?"

"We might be as late as five," I told her. "If we're going to be later than that, we'll call."

"Five o'clock, Mom. And Alice is driving because I wouldn't know the brake from the clutch." Another long pause. "Okay. Love you too. And Dad and God. Bye."

I waited until Amy was settled in the magazine

area just inside the library door. I pointed out the conference room across the hall.

"I'll be right over there, Amy. And if Student Jury isn't over by three thirty, I'll leave anyway and we'll go to the office."

"Right," Amy said. "And you're going to tell on him too."

"We're in this together," I promised.

17

Alice in Charge

I felt blood throbbing in my temples as I made my way to the conference room. And I almost stopped breathing when I walked in, because there was Dennis Granger.

I knew that teachers took turns as faculty adviser, but I felt sick as I listened to him tell Darien that he was substituting this time for the chemistry teacher. I could barely stand to look at him.

"You'll have to tell me how this works," he said cheerfully, glancing around the room. "Everybody's presumed innocent until declared guilty, right? And that's where you guys come in?"

I didn't even acknowledge him. Just settled myself in my chair and opened my bag, looking for a pen.

"Not exactly," I heard someone reply. "The offenders have already admitted to whatever it was they did; we simply decide the sentence. You know—the solution."

Mr. Granger sat down and pulled his chair up to the table. So far the faculty advisers had always sat off to one side, more observers than participants. Sleazebag looked as though he were here to take over.

He must have caught me studying him covertly because his eyes fastened on mine for a moment before I chickened out and looked away.

The case this time was a freshman who had been trashing one of the boys' restrooms. He'd been caught twice tossing wads of wet toilet paper at the ceiling where they stuck and dried, and the ceiling looked like the beginning of a hornet's nest. The kid was small for his age and wiry. He stood with his arms straight down at his sides, like he was about to be executed and deserved whatever he got.

"Is this new behavior for you, or did you do this kind of stuff in middle school?" Darien asked.

"I did it some," the boy answered.

"Ever get caught back in middle school?"

The boy shook his head.

"Do you do this in front of other guys, or when no one else is looking?" I asked.

"Mostly by myself," he said. "Sometimes with other kids . . . if they dare me." His voice was barely audible. This was probably the least serious case we'd had to deal with, and I was glad that we would be able to settle it quickly.

Dennis Granger leaned forward and rested his arms on the conference table. "Sometimes," he began, in a paternalistic tone, "people do destructive things simply because they know they can, and others do it for attention." I glared at him even though he wasn't looking at me.

"So which would you say it was?" Granger continued. "To see if you could get away with it or to get attention?"

The boy's face reddened a little, and he shrugged. "I don't know," he murmured.

Darien interrupted. "Excuse me, Mr. Granger, but this is Student Jury. We're supposed to ask the questions and impose the penalty."

Mr. Granger looked annoyed for a minute, then smiled and waved one hand as though to excuse himself and pulled back away from the table. "I guess I'm just here for decoration," he joked.

When the school secretary escorted the boy out of the room to await our verdict, it took us only a few minutes to talk it over.

"This seems pretty cut-and-dried to me," said Darien. "An 'experience-the-consequences' sort of thing. He did the damage, he undoes it."

"Does the school want him up on a ladder unsticking those wads of paper, though?" Kirk asked. "Is there an insurance factor here?"

"The school would be liable if he fell," Murray said. We looked at Mr. Granger.

"I can check that out for you," he said.

"Nix the ladder," said Lori. "Give him a long pole with a sponge on the end. He needs a workout."

"Why not tell the custodian to get the materials together and the boy does the job?" said Murray.

We all agreed. As the boy was brought in again—Betty Free came first and held the door open for him—I caught sight of Amy in the background. She was standing in the doorway of the library, waiting for me to come out, and in the five seconds or so that the door was open—the boy was taking his time—she saw Dennis Granger sitting there at the table. I saw the surprise on her face, the way she stared at him, at me. And then the door closed.

I gathered up my stuff. What if she thought I had talked to Granger about what she'd told me? What if she left the building?

Darien read the penalty, and when the kid agreed that it was fair, I pushed back from the table, slinging the strap of my bag over my shoulder. Darien set a date, and Mrs. Free told the boy he could leave. He skedaddled like a frightened mouse, and I stood up, ready to go. But when the boy opened the door to go out, I was astonished to see Amy Sheldon walk in.

Her cheeks were flaming red. She stood at

one end of the long table and, in her high-pitched voice, announced too loudly, "I want to make a complaint."

Everyone turned.

"A complaint goes to the principal or vice principal first—," Darien began.

"No, I have to make it now, because what if nothing happens?" Amy said. She didn't look to the right or left, just straight at Darien.

"What's the problem, Amy?" someone asked.

I stood riveted to the floor as I heard Amy answer, "Yesterday when Mr. Granger was tutoring me, I got molested."

The school secretary stared at her, speechless.

"Now, Amy, what in the world . . . ?" Mr. Granger started, an incredulous look on his face.

She refused to even glance his way. Just stood there, tilting slightly to one side as though facing a hurricane gale, struggling not to blow over. If ever I admired anyone, I admired Amy Sheldon at that moment.

"That's what happened," she said. "I said he could kiss me, but I didn't want to take my clothes off."

"What?" said Mr. Granger.

The school secretary hastily got to her feet. "Amy, this is something we need to talk about with Mr. Beck," she said, putting one arm around her shoulder. "Let's go back to the office."

"We all know that she's disturbed," Mr. Granger said softly as he rose from his chair, but I was furious.

"What she's disturbed about is what happened to her in that room, Mr. Granger," I said. "And she deserves to be heard." The other kids turned toward me, openmouthed. "I'm going with her. We have an appointment with Mr. Beck at three thirty."

Mrs. Free looked at me in astonishment.

Dennis Granger continued to shake his head. "She has these fantasies," he said.

Mrs. Free guided Amy toward the hall. "I think I've got some apple cider in our little fridge," she said. "We'll have a cup while you wait."

Amy twisted around to look at me. "Did I do okay, Alice?" she asked, as though I had put her up to this. "Am I a good friend?"

Now everyone was staring.

"Absolutely," I told her. "I'm right behind you."

Mr. Granger had exited the conference room through another door by this time, but as Amy walked out with Mrs. Free, Darien turned to me. "What the hell was *that* about? Do you think she's serious?"

"Dead serious," I told him, and followed Amy down the hall.

Mr. Beck was still in his meeting when we

reached the office, but Mrs. Free invited us back to a little rest area near the copy machine and poured us each a cup of cider. My stomach felt jumpy so I took only a sip, but Amy gulped hers down and even drank another cup. As long as I was with her, she seemed to be relaxed, but I wasn't at all sure they'd take us seriously.

When Mr. Beck's door opened at last, I heard one of the clerks tell him that I had asked for an appointment.

"Now?" he said, and I saw him glance at the clock. "What about?"

She shrugged.

Mrs. Free stepped into his line of sight then. "Alice McKinley and Amy Sheldon are waiting back here," she told him. "I'll bring them in."

Mr. Beck was holding the door open for us as we walked into his office.

"What can I do for you girls?" he asked, closing the door behind us and motioning for us to sit down. But instead of taking his office chair, he sat on the edge of his desk, as though we all agreed that this wouldn't take long.

Amy looked at me.

"We're here to report that we were both molested by Dennis Granger," I said, a slight tremor in my voice.

Mr. Beck's face changed from casual friendliness to surprise, and his eyes grew intent, serious.

"This . . . happened today? To both of you?" he asked.

"No. It happened to Amy yesterday. But just recently I was getting a drink at a water fountain and Mr. Granger came up behind me. He . . . pressed up against me . . . in an inappropriate way."

Mr. Beck nodded slowly, and this time he stood up, went around his desk, and sat down, pulling a pen out of his jacket pocket. "Do you remember the day and the time?"

"I could figure it out by looking at a calendar and let you know. But it was right after gym. And there were other times I wasn't sure . . . when he brushed his hand against my breast . . . It didn't seem definite enough to report. But this last time I was sure."

Mr. Beck nodded again. "I'm glad you girls came to me. This was the right thing to do." He turned toward Amy and waited.

She was a little less confident when she told her story, and I saw Mr. Beck wince when she said she had kissed Mr. Granger. I tried to help fill in the gaps where I could—things she had told me but was leaving out now—and the principal asked me not to comment on anything I hadn't seen directly. Somehow—without the convulsive sobbing I had witnessed and Amy hiding her face and the front of her skirt—it came off as less offensive somehow, less of an assault, and I wondered if Mr. Beck was taking her seriously. But I needn't have worried because he listened patiently, and when she was through, he said, "Amy, this is a serious matter and your parents need to be in on the discussion. Would anyone be home now if I called?"

Amy looked apprehensive. "Dad will say, 'Amy, I am not pleased,' if he is in an important meeting."

"Well, this is important too," Mr. Beck said gently. "What about your mom?"

"She's home."

"I'm sure they'll want to know that we are doing our best to protect you while you're at school, and they'll want to know what happened," he said. "Let's see if we can reach your mother."

When he did, once Mrs. Sheldon said she'd drive right over, Mr. Beck turned to me. "Alice, I appreciate you coming in and telling your version of the situation. I think it would be better if Amy told her parents the story in her own words, so you may go. But I want you to know we take this very seriously."

I wasn't sure of anything. Would Amy's story fizzle out when her parents were there to hear it? Would they think I had put her up to it—exaggerated it somehow? And where was Sleazebag Granger while we were there in Beck's office? He certainly wasn't sticking around.

Suddenly I realized that *The Edge* was going to press tonight, at our usual five o'clock deadline.

I walked swiftly to the newsroom. It was my job to do a brief write-up of each Student Jury meeting—describing each case and the jury's recommendation—without naming names. Today the staff had held off on finalizing the paper until I could insert this last item.

I was the only one in the newsroom. Phil had left a note:

> Alice,
> Got an appointment with the
> dermatologist, so you're in charge.
> Ames is at a conference. Wrap it
> up and send to printer.

Phil and Sam would drive to the printer's early the next morning to pick up the printed papers and bring them to the newsroom, then I'd help divide them up and distribute the bundles around school.

I sat down at the computer, where the unfinished page was already open. Phil had left very little room, but under the Student Jury headline, I typed:

> The jury heard the case against a
> freshman student for vandalizing

> a boys' restroom. He was assigned
> the job of removing the paper wads
> he'd thrown at the ceiling. . . .

My heart beat faster, an almost painful thumping. There was space left for two or three more lines. My fingers moved again:

> Jury was approached by an
> unscheduled student who reported
> molestation . . .

I took several deep breaths to allow myself to continue:

> . . . in room 208 after school
> hours. Complaint was referred to
> Mr. Beck.
> —Alice McKinley, Student Jury

I felt perspiration trickle down my sides, my brain sending off sparks in my head. I went over the rules again about reporting jury activities. I hadn't named names. I hadn't used dates. But . . .

I had one finger on the DELETE key. I thought of Amy's reddened face. I thought of Dennis Granger's smug smile. I thought of the wet spot on the front of Amy's skirt. . . . Taking my finger off the DELETE key, I pressed SAVE instead. Then I typed *Final Copy* in the subject line of the e-mail and sent the file off to the printer.

At home I went around all evening in a little protective cocoon, telling myself, *You did the right thing*. But the fact that I didn't tell Dad or Sylvia about it meant I wasn't sure. I didn't have any particular reason for believing that the principal might not believe Amy's side of the story, but I felt rage toward Dennis Granger. Not just about what he had done to Amy—her confusion and embarrassment—but that he had walked out on her so quickly afterward and left her to deal with her feelings herself. I can imagine he said something like, *I just can't help myself, Amy—you're so sexy*. And I can imagine she didn't start crying until after he'd left. But he *did* leave her there alone, so eager was he to get out, and I wanted to smack him down. I wanted him to suffer.

I worked on a physics problem after dinner and read another chapter in history. Didn't call anyone, but I checked my e-mail a couple times, looked up a few friends on Facebook without posting anything, then put on my pajamas.

Phil called around nine thirty. "Paper put to bed okay?" he asked.

"Yeah. I sent it in."

"Did I leave you enough room for the Student Jury update?" he asked. "You didn't have to cut anything?"

"It was enough," I said. "I probably wrote too much, I don't know."

"If you didn't move anything around, you're okay. See you tomorrow. I'll try to get some other staffers to help distribute," he said.

"See you," I said.

When I realized I was reluctant to tell even Phil what had happened, I knew I may have made a mistake. But then I thought of Amy, and said, *It's done.*

I woke Thursday with a headache. Dad drove me to school. When I got to the newsroom, Phil and Sam were back from the printer's and were already dividing the newspapers into bundles. I took off my jacket to help. We left one copy on Miss Ames's desk, then set off in different directions to leave papers at each school exit, the auditorium, the office—anywhere they were visible and students could pick them up.

We met Miss Ames as we were making the rounds. "Right on time!" she said when she saw us. "How did things go yesterday?"

"No problem," said Phil. "Alice did the wrap-up, and the papers were waiting at the printer's."

"Wonderful," Miss Ames said. "Did you leave some for the office?"

I nodded.

Phil and I went down to ground level and left newspapers at both entrances to the gym and at the science labs. When we went back up to the first floor, the halls were already filling with students, and the noise and laughter grew louder as we reached the top of the stairs. Most of the papers by the auditorium had already been taken, so we left another pile. We were in the east corridor, about halfway to the band room, when we heard the click of heels on the floor behind us.

"Alice?" Miss Ames called. "Phil?"

We turned and I felt my throat constrict.

Her face was stiff. No, furious. There was a tremor in her voice, she was so angry. "Who okayed that story about Student Jury?" she demanded.

"Student Jury?" Phil hadn't even read it yet.

"I . . . did," I said.

She stared at me with a look I'd never seen before. "What . . . in . . . the . . . world . . . were . . . you . . . *thinking*?" she demanded.

Phil stared at me, nonplussed.

My mouth was suddenly so dry that my tongue stuck to my teeth. "I thought . . . I was supposed to report everything that happened. I didn't . . . use names."

"You reported a matter that wasn't even supposed to be handled by Student Jury! I just talked to Betty Free, and she had no idea you were going to write that up."

Phil was scrambling to open one of the papers and find it.

Miss Ames waited coldly as he scanned the paragraph. He blinked and read it again. *"Ouch!"* he said, and gave me a sympathetic but pained look. "That's . . . uh . . . Granger's classroom, isn't it?"

"We're waiting for Mr. Beck to come in. He's meeting this morning with Amy Sheldon's father." She turned on me. "This was so *totally* uncalled for, Alice. So completely unnecessary."

I tried to defend myself. "Miss Ames, I didn't use Granger's name."

"You used the room number, Alice."

"But . . . it could have been someone else—a student even."

"The inference is there, regardless."

The bell for first period rang, and the halls began to empty.

"Should we go back and try to pick up all the papers we left around?" Phil asked.

Miss Ames shook her head. "Too late for that." She stopped and looked at me again. "Alice, I am so, *so* disappointed in you."

18

Change

I would rather have been slapped than to hear those words from our adviser.

I'd worked so hard for *The Edge*, moving up from roving reporter to features editor over the last four years. I so loved my job. And now . . . I remembered the sayings we had posted around the journalism room—Jefferson's statement that if he were asked to choose between "a government without newspapers or newspapers without a government, I should not hesitate a moment to prefer the latter"; Emerson's comment that it's not what lies behind us or ahead of us that counts as much as what lies within us; and the saying, "When in doubt, leave it out." I had been so full of doubt when I typed up that story that it was practically bleeding all over the keyboard. Somehow I'd known I was going too far, and yet . . .

Miss Ames walked away, and Phil turned to me. "Jeez, tell me what happened!" he said.

I told him how Amy had been waiting for me in the library and had seen Dennis Granger there with the jury. How she had come into the room and announced that he had molested her.

"Oh, man!" said Phil. "And you think it really happened?"

"I'm sure of it," I told him, and explained what I'd seen when I found Amy crying in Granger's classroom.

As the morning went on, though, I began to feel even more defensive. It *had* happened. Since when did I have to get permission from the office to report facts? Maybe this was something the students *should* find out about. Maybe this was a case where the faculty would try to protect one of their own. Maybe Jefferson would have said that if he had to choose between the faculty or *The Edge*, he'd choose our newspaper! I felt a little better.

I was called to the office around noon, and two policemen were there. Mr. Beck told me that Amy had given her side of the story to her parents and to the officers; would I now tell them what, if anything, I had observed of the incident? I repeated exactly what I had seen and what Amy had told me, as accurately as I could.

"And neither of you reported it to anyone on Tuesday?" one of the officers asked.

"I begged her to go to Mr. Beck or to tell her parents, and I'd made up my mind that if she didn't do it by today, I would. She agreed to wait for me in the library yesterday so we could go to the office together. Then . . . she saw Mr. Granger in the conference room—he was subbing for the chemistry teacher on Student Jury—and decided to report it there, I guess."

"You didn't expect that? You hadn't suggested it?"

"No!" I said emphatically. "She surprised us all. I didn't even know Mr. Granger would be there."

An officer was taking notes as I talked. "And you've reported inappropriate behavior toward yourself by Dennis Granger?"

"Yes," I said, and described again what had happened at the drinking fountain.

"You didn't report it then?"

"No. Things had happened before sort of like that—I wasn't sure. The way he brushes up against girls. That kind of thing."

"Thank you, Alice," Mr. Beck said when the questions were over. "You've been very helpful. This has been difficult, I know, but I do hope you'll keep this conversation confidential. It's unfortunate that other members of the Student Jury heard the charge and that it was mentioned in *The Edge*, but I assure you that we will follow through on this. You do understand that we want to make sure of our facts before we put a teacher's job and reputation in jeopardy? I trust we can count on your maturity as a senior not to discuss it further with anyone until the matter's resolved."

"Yes," I told him. "You can."

Kids did ask about it, of course, and everyone speculated, rightly, that it was probably Dennis Granger who did it. When asked, I simply said that I didn't know the outcome and that it would probably be in the county paper at some point. What was obvious was that Mr. Granger didn't come to school on Friday or the following week, either.

What I was most afraid of, since there were no witnesses to the act itself, was that Sleazebag would somehow convince the authorities that none of this had happened, that Amy was good at inventing stories, and so forth. That I, as her friend, had got caught up in the drama too.

But in the days that followed, Amy seemed more sure of herself, more confident. When kids gave her knowing, mocking smiles as they passed in the hallway, she interpreted them as a show of support, even though they weren't supposed to know that she was involved.

"You know what?" Amy told me. "Mom and Dad believe me one hundred and fifty percent. And some other people, too."

"You have more friends than you think," I told her.

"Do you remember when Jill accused Mr. Everett of coming on to her?" Pamela asked me at lunch as we sat on the floor outside the cafeteria, the seniors' favorite spot for lunch when the weather's bad and we have to eat inside.

"That was so scary," said Liz. "Everybody's favorite teacher, and we didn't know whether he'd be back or not."

"If Dennis Granger never comes back, I don't think anyone would miss him," said Pamela.

They looked at me, but they knew by now that I could tell them nothing.

Miss Ames was tight-lipped and all-business around me. She didn't fire me and she didn't mention the matter again. But you could tell there was a pall over the newsroom, that Phil and I had lost some of her respect and confidence—me, for writing up the incident in the first place, and Phil, for not reading the final proof. Whether Granger was found guilty or innocent, I had overstepped the boundary of good journalism.

"Oh, it'll blow over," Phil said comfortingly. "I wish you'd have run it by me, though, before it went to press. I called you, remember, and you didn't even mention it."

"Would you have worded it differently?" I asked. "If I hadn't included the room number, everyone would have asked."

"Maybe this is hindsight, but I think I would have told you not to include any of it. Like Miss Ames said, it wasn't a case for Student Jury. It was irrelevant."

He was right. The point was that I was furious with Dennis Granger and had included that room number *wanting* to hurt him.

A promise was a promise, though, and I didn't even tell Dad or Sylvia about it. Sylvia might accidentally mention it at her school, and it would travel like lightning. I'd wait till it all came out in the newspapers. More difficult yet, I didn't tell Patrick.

When he called, he seemed surprised I was home. "After I punched in your number, I told myself you'd still be at school, wrapping up the paper, or working for your dad, you've been so busy lately. How's it going?"

"Just a weary week. All sorts of hassles at the newspaper and the usual rush at the store," I told him. "What's happening at the Hog Butcher for the World?" (Taking my cue from Carl Sandburg.)

"Haven't butchered any hogs lately," Patrick said. "It's too cold here even for hogs."

"That cold already?" I asked.

"This is Chicago. You walk along the lake, you almost get blown over. I hate to think what it will be like in February."

"All I can think about is how wonderful it was in July," I told him. "The beach was beautiful."

"Yeah, well, now there are whitecaps on the water."

"I wish I was there to keep you warm," I told him.

"That would help," said Patrick.

He asked if there was anything new. I told him Jill and Justin broke up, and he was as surprised as the rest of us.

"Any idea why?"

"His mom, Jill says. It's a 'your mom or me' kind of thing."

"I guess if you're still sleeping at home and eating home cooking, you've got to choose Mom," Patrick said. And then, "This is going to sound like an awkward transition, Alice, but I've got some bad news. Well, sort of, I guess."

I didn't move. Didn't breathe. Something about his mother? Something about breaking up?

"I just couldn't bring myself to tell you earlier. . . ."

"Patrick, what *is* it?" I said, almost angrily, I was so anxious. I didn't need any more problems in my life.

"Mom and Dad have decided to move to Wisconsin to be close to his brother. They found a house when we were there at Thanksgiving."

My brain just couldn't seem to compute this. I knew Patrick had an uncle. Knew that Mr. and Mrs. Long often vacationed at his home in Wisconsin. If Patrick was going to college out of state anyway, did it really matter that—?

His *home*! His home would be in Wisconsin. He wouldn't be coming back here.

"W . . . when?" I asked in such a small, pitiable voice that I didn't recognize it as mine.

"Over Christmas. They want me to help sort through stuff when I come home for the holidays. The movers come on December twenty-eighth."

I was crying into the telephone. I felt the tears on my fingers.

"Alice?" Patrick said gently.

"Oh, Patrick!" I wept.

"I know," he said. "I felt the same way when they told me. But . . . I'm in college now. I wouldn't be home a lot anyway, and Dad's not as strong as he used to be. I can understand he'd want to be near family."

"And . . . and your mom?"

"She says she'd be happy wherever Dad wants to go."

We talked some more—the reasons, the details—but most of it slid by me. All I could think about was Patrick's empty house. Of Patrick going to Wisconsin now on spring and summer breaks.

"I . . . won't ever see you!" I cried.

I could tell he was smiling when he answered, "Well, you could always invite me to your prom."

"Of course! You know you're invited!"

"Well, I'll see you then. And I'll be back for Christmas in just a few weeks. We'll squeeze in every spare moment."

We each lingered over our conversation until we were tired out.

"Good night, Alice," he said.

"Good night, Patrick." I slowly pressed END on my cell phone and lay facedown on my bed. I felt as though the world were whirling on ahead of me and I'd been left far behind.

In the locker room after gym the next day, I told my friends.

"The Longs are moving to Wisconsin," I said.

All chatter stopped.

"What?" said Pamela. "When?"

"A few days after Christmas. Patrick's coming home to help them pack. Mr. Long wants to be near his brother."

"Oh, Alice!" said Liz, sitting down with a shoe in one hand.

"And Patrick's going with them?" Pamela asked.

"Duh!" said Gwen.

"I mean, he's at the University of Chicago and—" Even Pamela realized how dumb her question seemed. "Yeah. Where would he stay if he came back here on spring break?" Then she brightened mischievously. "You've got a big house now, Alice. What about Lester's old room?"

"Don't even think it," I said. "Dad would be patrolling the hall all night."

"He wasn't so strict with Les, from what I heard—all the girlfriends," said Pamela. "How many dozen were there?"

"Not in our house, there weren't. Well, with a few exceptions," I told them.

Liz looked about as sad as I felt. "If he comes home at Christmas to help them pack . . . and they move . . . you may never see Patrick again!"

"Liz!" the others chorused together, giving her signals with their eyebrows.

"Where there's love, there's a way," Pamela declared, and slowly the conversation drifted to Jill and Justin, how long they'd been battling his parents in order to stay together—Jill had, anyway. What reassurance was there in that? I wondered. Look how that turned out!

19

Conference

Toward the end of that week, almost everyone in school knew what had happened in room 208. The names leaked out from the other jury members, a substitute was hired in Dennis Granger's place, and when someone actually walked up to Amy in the hall and asked, "Was it you?" Amy answered, "I only said he could kiss me."

A letter went out to parents that the administration had zero tolerance for this—that an adult, and especially an adult in a position of authority, is always the person responsible.

But if there were any doubts about Amy's side of the story, they disappeared when a second girl came forward to report that Mr. Granger had groped her in a hallway after a late-afternoon band rehearsal, and in checking out her story, it was discovered that part of it had been caught on a security camera a month ago.

Amy became a sort of cult heroine. Even

kids who joked about her social awkwardness were recounting her story, heard secondhand, of course, of how she had simply walked into the Student Jury room and announced that a teacher had molested her—in front of the very teacher. Her candidness, her ingenuousness, became her virtue. Kids high-fived her in the hallways. Told her she was brave, which she was. Honest, which she was. "Way to go, Amy!" they said to her with a smile, and she thrived on all the attention.

"You know what?" she said to me. "Mom and Dad were going to put me in another school, but I said no, I'm a roving reporter, and they said I could stay. Isn't that good, Alice?"

"It's terrific," I told her.

"And now that another girl had almost the same thing happen to her, it's not just a crazy story by a crazy person, is it?"

"Definitely not, and you were never crazy, Amy," I said.

I had thought that with a second girl coming forward with her story, and a police investigation begun, I would be exonerated somehow. I had been raked over the coals for including it in my write-up; Phil had been reprimanded for not reading my final copy; and Miss Ames was in the hot seat with Mr. Beck for allowing *The Edge* to go to press without her okay on everything in it. Didn't Granger's suspension prove I'd been right to do it? Shouldn't I be, like, *congratulated* for breaking the story?

Miss Ames called a conference of the four editors of the paper—Phil, Sam, Tim, and me. "We need to think about what happened last week," she said. "We need to clear the air, go over our policies, and make sure we're all on the same page. I think it might help if we begin where it started and explore exactly what Alice was thinking when she did the write-up. I'm not talking blame here. Let's just try to examine this critically and see where we could have made a different choice." She stopped and turned toward me, waiting.

What more could I say? "Well," I began, "one of my jobs, since I'm a member of the Student Jury, is to write up what goes on at each session, without using names. I guess I thought that's what I was doing."

"Okay. Fair enough. Let's start there." Miss Ames turned toward the others. "If some parent had arrived for a parent-teacher conference during your session and said they thought they were supposed to meet in the room you were using and one of you directed them to the office, would you have felt it necessary to include that in your write-up?"

I thought that over. "No."

"Wasn't Amy coming in to report something that should have gone to the principal the same thing?"

"Well, not exactly. She was reporting an offense that happened in our school, and as far as she was concerned, the jury deals with offenses," I said.

"Even though Betty Free immediately told her that the matter should go to the principal?"

I didn't answer, but Sam took my point of view. "Alice might have had the feeling that even if the complaint went to the office, there would be a cover-up."

"That's a pretty negative way to look at our school." Miss Ames seemed surprised. "Why would you think it might be covered up?"

We were all quiet for a few moments, and Miss Ames let us take our time. Finally I said, "I don't think the administration's been moving very fast on some of the stuff that's been happening with Bob White and Company, whoever they are—the white supremacy stuff."

Miss Ames didn't answer, just listened. "Okay," she said finally. "Point taken. But let me ask this: In the write-ups you've done about other people who were brought before the jury, did you include their locker numbers? Their homerooms?"

I could tell where this was going. "No," I said.

"Yet you reported the room number where the incident took place, and most people know that this is the room Dennis Granger uses."

"Yes," I said.

"Alice, looking at this with absolute honesty, did you have any hesitation at all in reporting the story the way you did?"

I wanted, of course, to deny it. But as the others waited, I remembered my nervousness as I'd hesitated over the DELETE key. Remembered the pounding of my heart when I'd pressed SEND.

"Yes," I said. "Not about reporting what happened, exactly, but about including the room number."

"Yet you put it in. Why?"

"Because I . . . I was just so mad at Granger. Amy was so vulnerable. And she was so humiliated, as though she were the one at fault."

"But why *didn't* you run it by me first?" Phil asked. "You could have called."

"You were at the doctor's."

"You've got my cell number."

"Or you could have called me," said Miss Ames.

"Phil said you were at a conference."

"I was home by then, but if not, you could have left a message."

"We're supposed to have the final copy at the printer's no later than five, so they can start running it before the day crew leaves," I said weakly, knowing full well that once in a while we don't make the deadline, but the printer usually still has our copies ready by noon the next day.

"You could have at least told me when I called you that night to check that the paper was all put to bed, Alice. You said everything was okay," Phil said.

Miss Ames leaned her arms on the table, her shoulders hunched. She looked tired. Even the scarf at her neck looked droopy. "The final responsibility for this paper rests with me because I'm faculty adviser," she said, "and I allowed the paper to go to press without my final okay, just as Phil did. I'm guilty as well. I trusted that Phil would do it for me, Phil trusted Alice, and Alice dropped the ball. This is a chance for all of us to look more seriously at our own responsibilities here at the paper."

"But . . . but doesn't the fact that the security camera caught Dennis Granger with that second girl . . . I mean, if anything, shouldn't the administration be grateful to *The Edge* that we smoked him out? If Amy hadn't reported him, and if I hadn't written about it—" I halted for a moment. "Isn't the responsibility of a newspaper to follow through on reports and rumors and see if there's a story behind them? Isn't that what reporters are supposed to do?"

"Yeah, but what if it turned out that Amy made the whole thing up?" put in Tim, playing devil's advocate now. "At the time you wrote it, you had every reason to suspect Granger did it. But a guy's still innocent until he's been proven guilty."

"So looking back," Miss Ames said, winding it up, "would you say that we were biased in our reporting? That deep down, we assumed Dennis Granger was guilty even before we'd got the full story? Before the other girl came forward with an accusation?"

"I think we could assume that. But now that he's confessed . . . ," said Phil.

"So the end justifies the means?" asked Sam.

We thought about that, too.

"I guess that's what it sounds like," I said. Then, turning to the others, "I want to apologize to the staff. I know that the rest of you are taking the blame along with me. And I know that I felt—even at the time—I was going too far. And I didn't call anyone because I didn't want anyone to overrule me. I was afraid that if I didn't out him, Granger would get off scot-free, that the administration would believe him, not Amy. But . . . if that had happened . . . then we'd have to decide what to do next. It wasn't my job to predict."

I would have liked Miss Ames better if we could have just ended the meeting there, but she got sort of sappy and had us all link arms around the conference table while she told us that even great newspapers make mistakes, but we were still a team, a good one, that we'd move on, and she knew we'd produce articles and reports that we could be proud of for the rest of the school year.

I decided I should probably stick with counseling, not journalism, when I got to college.

It's amazing, with all that was going on, I even remembered the Snow Ball. But when I awoke on Friday, with the newspaper stuff behind me, I threw my whole psyche into the evening ahead, and Sylvia came home early to do my hair. We piled it high on my head, with some fake green daisies with black centers. Sylvia had let out the side seams in the dress as far as they'd go and told me if I was still uncomfortable in it, she'd put in another zipper. But I'd lost a couple pounds in my worry over Amy, so the dress was still tight, but okay.

And so I went to the Snow Ball.

Not all the guys wore tuxes; a lot of them were in suits and ties, and Daniel wore his brother's sport coat, with sleeves that reached his knuckles. But there he stood when I opened the door, and handed me a bouquet he'd picked up at the Giant. He was embarrassed because he'd found out too late the flowers were supposed to be in a corsage. I told him I'd appreciate them even more because they'd last longer this way, and he grinned.

Keeno and Liz were waiting out in the SUV with Pamela and Louie, and we went to pick up Gwen and Austin.

Daniel wasn't quite as spontaneous and extroverted as he'd been at the Homecoming Dance—awed, I guess, by all the formality, as well as by the large snowflakes that hung from a starry sky in the school gym. Astonished at the fake snowdrifts heaped along the walls and the rotating sparkles, like snowflakes themselves, that a strobe light cast on the dance floor.

"In America," he said as we danced the two-step, "there is real snow on the outside and imagination snow on the inside. It is amazing."

I laughed at his pleasure in the light dusting of snow we'd had the evening before. "You haven't seen anything yet," I told him. "Wait until there's enough to make a snowball. That's when it really gets interesting."

The big surprise of the evening was that Jill and Justin were together again, and when they made their grand entrance, they were the center of attention for the rest of the evening. They danced so close together, we felt the dance patrol would be after them to break it up—Jill's leg entwined around Justin's, he with one knee between her thighs. Pamela guessed that maybe the breakup itself had been a hoax, but Jill looked ravishing in a white dress with a low back—a very low back—and I had to smile when I sensed that Daniel was afraid to let his eyes linger at all in that direction.

"I do not know how to tell my brothers back in Africa how it is in the United States of America," he said when we gathered at the refreshment table. "Everything is so different here, they would not even imagine it. 'No, it cannot be,' they would say. Snowflakes from a light in the ceiling? What are snowflakes? What are corsages? What are the things you eat from boxes—the cereal? So many things from boxes. All are very strange to me. And salads!" he went on, getting warmed up. "In Sudan we cook our vegetables. We do not eat them raw like goats. 'Here they eat grass!' I will tell my brothers!"

We laughed.

"You've got to put that in your next story for *The Edge*," I told him.

"But what about us?" Liz asked him. "I've never seen a live camel. I've never seen a date tree. It works both ways."

"And I don't know a foreign language," I said. "I can't speak both English and Dinka."

Daniel grinned. "So we should trade for a year—your school with a refugee camp. I am sometimes feeling bad that I am here in America and my friends are still in a camp."

All the girls in our group managed to dance

with Daniel during the evening, and toward the end he loosened up a little and tried some of the fast numbers first with me, then Pamela.

Just like at proms, a lot of girls came in groups by themselves, and some of the guys did the same, mixing or not as the evening wore on and things grew less formal. Girls took their shoes off and danced in bare feet, and the guys shed their jackets.

The eight of us left the dance an hour early and went to a Mexican restaurant for a midnight supper. Daniel loved the spicy food, and we all chipped in on the bill.

"What's the story with Jill and Justin?" Liz asked. "Anyone know anything?"

"I talked to Jill in the ladies' room and asked if the breakup had been just a trial separation," Pamela told us. "She said a trial, maybe, but that they'd started talking about getting back together sometime over Thanksgiving weekend, and now they're even closer than before."

"Maybe Justin inherits some of his grandfather's money when he's eighteen and they're going to elope," said Gwen.

"Maybe he'll leave home and move in with Jill and her parents," said Liz.

"Who's Jill? Who's Justin?" asked Louie.

"A couple who's been going together since Adam and Eve," Pamela answered. "We're taking bets on how it's all going to come out."

When Daniel walked me to the porch after Keeno dropped me off, the others undoubtedly watching from the car, he very courteously shook my hand and thanked me for accepting his invitation to the dance.

"I had a wonderful time. Thanks for inviting me," I said.

He asked again how long the flowers he had given me would keep.

"For several days, I'm sure of it," I said.

"If they begin to wilt . . . if you do not want them any longer then," he said uncertainly, "I will give them to my mother."

"Tell you what," I said. "I'll keep them till Monday, and then I'll give them back and she'll have a chance to enjoy them too."

Daniel beamed at his own cleverness.

Patrick called me on Sunday to see how the dance had gone.

"It was fun," I told him. "A bunch of us traded dresses."

"And . . . Daniel?"

"He didn't wear a dress."

Patrick laughed. "He put the moves on you?"

"A perfect gentleman from the beginning of the evening to the end. Oh, Patrick, I can't bear the thought of you moving."

"Then let's don't think about it, Alice. Let's think about my coming home at Christmas."

"I spend ninety percent of my time thinking about that already," I told him.

Sam had taken some good photos at the dance, and he printed out a half dozen to display in the showcase outside the auditorium on Monday. There were Jill and Justin, glued together, eyes closed; Keeno and Liz, their feet blurred in a fast dance; Daniel and me, dancing demurely, smiling at each other; Phil and his date; a couple of freshmen. . . .

Little crowds stopped at the showcase throughout the day, wondering which shots would appear in the next issue of the paper and how many more had been taken.

I helped out at the Melody Inn that evening. Now that the Snow Ball was over and I was on friendly terms with Miss Ames again, I discovered that the rock in the pit of my stomach still hadn't gone away. Each time I thought of Patrick moving to Wisconsin, my mind went into overdrive, thinking up all the reasons I could give him for this not to happen.

His parents had been living in Silver Spring for . . . seven . . . eight years? Didn't they have a lot of friends here they'd leave behind? Didn't they belong to a church? Did they really want to experience Midwest winters while we usually had mild winters here in Maryland? And what about tornadoes?

What about their house? I'll bet they wouldn't be able to sell their house in this market! How could they buy another in Wisconsin if they couldn't sell this one? And how could they ever pack in time?

A woman was standing at the counter with three CDs she wanted to buy and I hadn't even noticed. "I'm sorry," I said quickly, taking her credit card. "Too much on my mind."

"It's that time of year," she said generously. "Have a good Christmas."

Kay's boyfriend came to pick her up when we closed at nine.

"Where are you spending Christmas? Will your parents still be away?" I asked her.

She put one arm around the red-haired guy, who reminded me of Patrick. "Kenny's parents invited me over," she said.

"Lucky!" I told her.

Les called just as I was going to bed that night, to say that he had tickets to his graduation for all three of us.

Yikes! I thought. I'd forgotten all about it. Maybe one of the most important days in Lester's life, and it was getting lost in all the tribulations of my own.

"We'll be there, Les," I said. "How many people are graduating?"

"Two thousand seven hundred and fourteen," he said.

I sank down on my bed and tried to figure out how long it would take twenty-seven hundred people to cross a stage, one at a time, and listen to a graduation speech to boot.

"I can't wait," I said.

"Hey, I'll have to sit through yours too," said Les.

I got to school early Tuesday to turn in a paper that was already overdue—the teacher had said she'd accept it if I got it in her box by seven o'clock. I made it, glad to check one more thing off my to-do list, and turned down the hallway to my locker.

My eye caught something dangling from the handle. As I got closer, I saw that it was a little ceramic bride and groom, the kind that appear on top of a wedding cake. The groom's face had been smeared with black ink, and the couple had been suspended from the locker handle by a thin piece of brown string, braided into a miniature noose. The loop was bound tightly around the neck of the bride.

20

Confrontation

I was afraid to even touch them. Terrified, I looked around to see if anyone was watching, anyone who might have done this, but the corridor was empty. A girl and a guy appeared at the far end of the hall, their arms around each other. They paused to kiss. No one else was near.

Saliva gathered at the back of my throat, but I didn't swallow. I got the message, all right—the photo in the showcase from the Snow Ball. I stared at the figures of the bride and groom. If anyone was watching, I didn't want to appear scared.

I jerked hard at the string, but it didn't break. I reached inside my bag and took out my nail file, then sawed away at the cord and jerked it again. This time the string broke. The couple fell to the floor, chipping a piece off the groom's foot. Picking the pieces up, I dropped them into my bag and walked quickly to the library just to have a place to go, my breath coming fast. I wanted to be near people. I didn't know what to do with the bride and groom or whom to tell. Was this just a joke or a threat? I wondered if I should have touched them. Perhaps there were fingerprints. I sat at a table and pretended I was doing homework.

Don't act afraid, I told myself. *Treat it as a silly prank.* But another voice said, *Tell security.* Yeah, right. I had already stirred up one hornet's nest. There would be another "word from the principal" over the sound system. Perhaps another letter from the editor in our paper. Just like Amy's incident with Dennis Granger, the story would be all over school, and the one thing I didn't want *anyone* to think was that I was afraid, even though I was shaking.

Who was doing this? How could I go day after day wondering if I was passing that person in the hall, sitting beside that person in class? Waiting in line in the cafeteria in front of the person who had put a symbolic rope around my neck? How many people were in on it? Maybe a lot more than I thought.

It was cold, with an icy rain that pinged against the windows during morning classes. *Nobody wants to go Christmas shopping in this*, I thought, recalling that Dad had checked the forecast at breakfast that morning, wanting cold days to remind people it was December already; clear days, to draw them outdoors; and a little dusting of snow, perfect for putting them in a Christmasy mood. Instead, the ping of sleet played only a single tune: *Stay home.*

Maybe I was thinking about Christmas right then because I knew Patrick would be helping his parents pack up for their move when he came home. Maybe I was thinking about Patrick because if he hadn't graduated a year early—if he were still in school—he'd protect me. I could show him the wedding cake decoration at the bottom of my bag, and he'd drive me to and from school each day, wait for me at the end of last period, be with me in the halls. . . .

By mid-afternoon the sleet had stopped and the ceramic bride and groom were still in my bag. I tried to focus on some long-neglected schoolwork. I spent all of my free period back in the library researching the Marshall Plan after World War II. I'd found some material on the Internet, but the teacher also assigned one of two books to read about it, and I was scanning the history section to see if either book was in.

Daniel was hunched over a stack of books in a study kiosk near the back. Phil was there too, at one of the computers, and several other people were hard at work. The library had a new policy regarding noise and conversation. You could meet friends and chat before or after school, but it had adopted Amtrak's "Quiet Car" policy during school hours. Most of the time I appreciated this, but when I noticed Curtis Butler searching for a book a few feet away from me, I wished I could have a conversation with him. Just sit in the soft chairs near the back and ask why he didn't come to GSA meetings anymore. What happened to the Safety Council? Who, if anyone, was threatening him here on campus?

If he remembered me, he gave no sign of it. He took one book from a high shelf and sat down with it for a few minutes to search its pages. I was still standing at the shelves when he got up again to put it back.

I glanced up as he stretched to slip the book onto the highest shelf, and as the cuff of his jacket pulled back slightly on his arm, I saw a barbed-wire tattoo forming a bracelet around his wrist. And just below the bracelet, a dark double eight tattoo.

Curtis picked up his bag from the floor, slung it over his shoulder, and left the library.

Was it possible?

I sank down in the same chair where he had been sitting and waited for my breathing to slow. Of course! He came to a few GSA meetings because he was scoping us out, wanting to see how many came, who the "homos" were. And the "Safety" Council? Disbanded because they wanted to practice martial arts. And hadn't I remembered Curtis and some other guys at the Homecoming Dance, watching from the sidelines when the girls were laughing it up, teaching Daniel some steps? As for the Snow Ball, no one had to attend to know that I was Daniel's date for the evening, not after Sam put up that photo in the showcase. My mind kept leapfrogging over what I knew for sure and what I only conjectured.

I stood up and scanned the high shelf for the book Curtis had been reading, hoping I could easily spot it. It rested at an angle against the one next to it, and by standing on tiptoe, using another book as a tool, I was able to edge it forward and catch it when it fell: *The Rise and Fall of the Third Reich.*

When Phil left the library, I followed him into the hall and breathlessly told him about the bride and groom ornament, my suspicions about Curtis.

"Alice, I think it's time to do something," he said.

"What? Tell Beck?"

"I don't know, but you ought to report it. He

could at least get security to keep an eye on the guy. And maybe on you."

"We have sixteen hundred students, Phil, and three security guards."

"Well, what do *you* propose? You're leading with your chin again, this time by keeping this to yourself."

"I'm telling you about it, aren't I?" I leaned against the wall and stared down the long row of lockers. "It's just . . . what if I'm wrong? I mean, I talked to the guy when he first showed up at GSA. He was friendly enough. I've seen him around, and he didn't seem violent or anything. Maybe he was tattooed by the gang. Maybe he was reading that book to try to find out what makes racists tick. Maybe he's scared to talk to me. I don't know. . . ."

The bell rang.

"Look, I've got to get to class," Phil said. "You busy after school?"

"Not right away. I'm going to work for my dad at six . . . or whenever I get there."

"You know that doughnut shop in the little strip mall across from the Giant? Can you meet me there after school to talk about this? I've got to return a form to the band room, but I'll be there around three," Phil said.

I said that I would, and made my way to gym. I found myself looking at arms, necks, even the legs of the girls in their gym shorts, looking for double eight tattoos. The fact that there might be girls in the group made it all the scarier somehow. Maybe they were just groupies. Girls who would do anything to get chummy with the guys. Or maybe they were true believers, who knew?

We volleyed the ball back and forth over the net, dipping and dodging to keep it in the air. No double eights on the court that I could see.

Daniel was at the drinking fountain after I'd showered and left the gym. He said the water was too cold. He always held it in his cheeks for a second or two before swallowing.

"You're like a camel," I told him. "All that water."

"Why do they put it in machines that ice it?" he wondered. "It does not even have taste when it's that cold. My teeth hurt from your water."

"Maybe we ought to buy you a canteen," I joked.

He walked with me to the next corridor. "When the weather gets very, very cold here— when the snows come—does the cold kill?"

"Only if you're out in the snow and get lost or something. If you can't take shelter and you're not dressed for it. We won't let it happen to you, Daniel," I promised. "By the way, is everything all right? No more notes or stuff in your locker?"

"No," he said. "People are kind to me. If they do not speak or smile, that's all right. There are very many people in this school. It is like a city. Not everyone speaks or smiles at you in a city."

I had nothing to do at school after the last bell rang at two thirty, but I remembered there was a dollar store over near the doughnut shop. I could use some notebook paper and eyeliner.

There was no sidewalk leading out from the east side of the school, and though the rain and sleet had stopped, the wind whipped at the scarf around my neck. I decided to take a shortcut and started across the football field. My feet made crunching sounds as I stepped on frozen grass.

Buses were pulling away from the front entrance, heading out in the other direction. I could hear cars starting up in the student parking lot, everyone leaving at the same time, the noise getting dimmer the farther I walked.

Off in the distance traffic whizzed by the strip mall. The football field was empty except for a couple of guys sitting on the second row of the bleachers, smoking, hoods turned up on their jackets. The shriek of a crow flying overhead brought answering heckles from the woods off to one side.

I wished I'd worn gloves, and I alternated hands, one keeping my scarf from blowing away, the other warming in my jacket pocket.

One of the boys noticed me and lowered his cigarette—forbidden on campus.

Don't worry, I thought, *I'm not about to report you*, and I plowed on, bucking the wind. Was that doughnut shop where I thought it would be, or was I thinking of another strip mall? I wondered. Phil had said it was across from the Giant, but wasn't there an Exxon station on that corner?

The second guy stood up. He was looking in my direction, but I couldn't see his face. For ten or fifteen seconds he seemed to be watching me approach, then he stepped over the bleacher in front of him and started forward. The other followed. They walked steadily in my direction, their pace deliberate, shoulders hunched. Too late, I recognized the face of Curtis Butler.

Fight or flight? I could feel the pounding inside my chest, the throbbing in my temples. Every nerve came alive, every muscle tensed. My legs, cold as they were, trembled slightly and my mouth was as dry as chalk.

There was no one else here. No road with steady traffic. No sidewalk with passing students. I could never outrun both of them, even if I turned and headed back. I was probably everything the racists were against: I supported gay rights, mingled with lesbians, dated a black guy. . . .

I remembered some of the things I'd read about—stories of what some white supremacists would do to "make an example of" someone. A storm trooper kicking a Hispanic woman in the face, a gay beaten to death, a homeless alcoholic stomped with steel-toed boots . . . all in a crazed expression of "keeping America pure."

As they neared, in a desperate effort to deflect them, I heard my own voice call out, "Hey, Curtis! I've been looking for you." My chest hurt with the pounding of my heart.

He slowed, paused, then stopped as I came up to him.

"Yeah?" he said coldly, hands in his pockets. "What about?"

I struggled to keep my voice from shaking. "I'd like to ask a favor."

The large boy beside him glanced at Curtis, then back at me. The hood had slipped partly down his head, and I could see that he had blond hair, a somewhat bent nose, deep-set gray eyes.

Curtis's eyes narrowed. "What kind of favor?"

"Thought you might do an article for us about your group."

There was an edgy silence. Curtis picked a piece of tobacco off his tongue, then spit. "What group you talking about?"

"The double eight, or whatever you call your-selves. I know there's a lot you want to say, so I'm offering you a front-page spot instead of the notes and stuff you've been leaving around."

Curtis shifted his weight to his other foot and studied me, eyes staring unblinking into mine. "Why you talking to me about this?"

I shrugged to hide the shivering. "Who *should* I be talking to?" He didn't answer.

"This the girl who goes for black guys?" asked his friend.

Curtis ignored him. "Who put you up to this?" he asked me.

"No one. C'mon, I get original ideas once in a while."

"What's the catch?"

"Only that other kids can respond, and we'll print their replies in the next issue, pro or con. But that shouldn't bother you. This is your chance. And you've got to sign your real name. No more 'Bob White.' That's better than trashing armbands and leaving a noose on my locker door."

"I didn't put that there," Curtis said quickly.

"You said you didn't care!" protested his friend.

"Shut up," said Curtis. He fished in his pocket for another cigarette and lit it. "I say whatever I want, I'd get kicked out."

"Not if you can write it without name-calling. You heard what Beck said: Every student has a right to free expression. You do believe in freedom, don't you?"

"For the people who founded the U.S. of A., yeah," said Curtis. "Not the ones who came after."

I decided not to argue the point here on a windy field with no help in sight. "So you'll do it? Write an article?"

Curtis shrugged and turned sideways, looking off into the distance.

"It would be short," I said. "About two hundred and fifty words. But you can say a lot in two hundred fifty words. Deadline noon tomorrow?"

"Front-page article? Just as I write it?"

"If you keep it clean."

"I'll think about it," said Curtis.

They walked on past me, and I continued toward the strip mall, perspiration trickling down my back, a desperate urge to pee. Any moment I expected to feel an arm around my neck from behind. But I didn't.

When I reached the doughnut shop, Phil was already there at one of the small tables.

"Alice!" he said when he saw me. "What's the matter?"

I was breathing hard and went immediately to the restroom. When I came back, I collapsed in the chair across from him. "I think my heart stopped temporarily. Actually, I've been scared half out of my mind." I was still breathing jerkily.

"*What?* What happened?"

"I just ran into Curtis Butler and one of his buddies on the football field. I was stupidly taking a shortcut. They were smoking on the bleachers and came toward me."

"Jeez, Alice! You were alone?"

I nodded. "I couldn't think of what to do, so I told Curtis I wanted him to write an article for *The Edge*."

Phil squinted in disbelief. "You . . . *what*?"

"It was fight or flight," I said. "I couldn't take on both of them."

Phil just sat there staring at me. Then, "What's he going to *say*? You trying to get us both booted off the staff?"

"I don't know. I told him this was his chance. To express himself, I mean."

"Alice, what exactly did you promise him?"

I took a deep breath. "Front page. Next issue. Two hundred and fifty words. But he has to use his real name and write it without racial slurs. I told him we'd publish the responses in the following issue."

Gradually, as Phil's stare became less fixed, I saw his shoulders begin to relax, his face to soften. Finally he said, "You know, it just might be the best idea you've ever had."

I don't know where I got the courage to face Curtis Butler as I did. Maybe from Amy's example.

When I told Miss Ames all that had happened and how I'd come to request the front-page article from Curtis, she smiled and shook her head in disbelief. "You just can't help saving the world, can you, Alice?"

"It was me I was trying to save," I told her. "It was all I could think of to do."

"Well, we don't know where this will lead. But we hadn't figured out until now who was behind all this, so you may have opened the door for some real dialogue here. Better than nooses hanging from lockers," she said.

I couldn't have agreed more.

21

Wrap-up

Our next-to-the-last issue before Christmas vacation:

> The staff of *The Edge* thinks it might be important to present a minority view from time to time and has therefore asked for a short essay from a junior student which follows below. It goes without saying that the beliefs presented here are neither those of the administration nor of the newspaper staff, but because there seems to be an undercurrent of anger in this school, we feel it might be helpful to get these views out in the open. Your responses will be published in our "Sound Off" column next week.
> —Alice McKinley, Features Editor

STANDING UP FOR THE WHITE RACE

by Curtis Butler

A lot of you may not agree with me, but I'm trying to save a dying race. The USA was created as a homeland for people of European descent and not as a melting pot or refuge for non-Europeans, because what we're becoming is a third world ghetto.

White people in their very own country get a raw deal. Africans come here and are treated like some kind of royalty—scholarships and free housing and food, and all they have to do is show up at school and dances. Mexicans sneak into the U.S. of A. and get the jobs that decent white Americans should have, and everybody knows that Jews get all the money, one way or another. Just look at the names of investment firms and you'll see they're all Jewish.

If our nation keeps this up, mixing together and even marrying, we are all going to end up the same color and not believing in God and probably not even having children because we'll all be homosexual.

I personally don't believe in violence because that only hurts our cause. I, and others like me, believe that white teenagers should band together—free of drugs, homosexuality, and race mixing, not believing the Zionist-controlled TV and radio. Our goal is to promote racial awareness and pride, and it's about time we started taking care of ourselves.

<u>Note from the Faculty Adviser</u>: If these, and opposing, views can be discussed without name-calling and slurs, if we can express emotion without violence, we can show the community that this is a school in the truest sense, where even ideas that are repugnant to many can be discussed as to their cause and resolution. It is the

> hope of the newspaper staff that
> prejudice—in the act of being
> examined and questioned—can be
> healed.
>
> —Shirley Ames

The day the paper came out, we felt as though we may have planted a time bomb in it. I'd had to edit Curtis's article, of course. I'd changed *Mexicanos* to *Mexicans*, and *mud-colored* to *the same color*.

Nobody knew what would happen, though. Miss Ames had alerted Mr. Beck and Mr. Gephardt, and we noticed there was an extra security man on duty that Thursday, just strolling around the halls. We didn't expect a rock through the window of the newsroom or anything, because it wasn't considered "cool" to get emotional, but those of us on the newspaper— and Miss Ames in particular—wondered if we'd done the right thing; if we'd started something we couldn't control.

Because of the noose threat, Phil and Tim and Sam made sure that one of them walked me to and from classes each day if I wasn't in a group. I noticed that Curtis went around school flanked by two buddies—one of them the guy I'd met out on the football field. There was a wary macho air about them, as though expecting trouble. But

Mr. Gephardt was everywhere, talking with everyone, and surprisingly, the day went off without incident.

A lot of kids hadn't read the article yet, of course, and of those who had, a lot looked upon it with ridicule. There were a few jeers, some condescending remarks, but so much was going on with Christmas coming up and semester finals to take that most of the kids probably dismissed it and moved on.

There was a lot going on in my life too besides school—Lester's graduation, for one. Why the U of Maryland thinks the weekend before Christmas is a good time to hold a graduation escapes me, but there we were in the Comcast Center—Dad, Sylvia, and me (and several ex-girlfriends of Lester's), cheering him on. I was coming down with a cold, but I would be at Lester's graduation if I had to crawl there on my hands and knees. I stuffed my bag with Kleenex and throat lozenges and waited for his turn on the stage.

We didn't know what Les would be able to do with a master's degree in philosophy, but it pleased me to see the pleasure and relief on his face when the dean read his name and shook his hand in congratulations.

"Way to go, Les!" I yelled amid the general applause, and Les grinned in my direction and waved.

"Les," Sylvia told him afterward, "I'm only your stand-in mom, but I'm as proud of you as a person can possibly be."

Dad hugged him, and Les hugged back. "It was a long road, but you made it," Dad said. "I knew you would."

"Then you're psychic, Dad, because I wasn't always sure," Les said.

We took him out to dinner at his favorite steak house, and I tried to think what the day would be like if Mom were here—what she'd say. She was tall, Les always told me. Strawberry blond hair, lots of it. She sang. She liked to laugh. To swim. To camp out and hike.

She'd be smiling, of course. Maybe she'd be sitting with her arm around Les. Or maybe she'd just lay one hand over his on the table. She'd probably have a funny story to tell us about Les when he was little, and maybe she'd have her other arm around me.

I wondered if Les was thinking of her just then. Wondered if Dad was thinking of her. And when he said, "Marie would have been so proud," I was sure of it.

Maybe more people read *The Edge* than we'd thought. We got so many responses to Curtis's article that we had to give "Sound Off" a full page in our last issue before Christmas. I knew we'd have even more waiting for us when we came back from winter break.

Miss Ames wrote the introduction:

> These are the first responses to Curtis Butler's essay in last week's *Edge*. We recognize that emotions run high on this subject, but we believe that as civilized people, any debate is preferable to keeping our feelings under wraps. We will take him at his word that he doesn't believe in violence. *The Edge* will print all responses as long as they are signed by students attending this school and do not resort to profanity, threats, or slurs. Your ability to write in this manner will demonstrate your maturity.
> —Shirley Ames, Faculty Adviser

> Was that essay by Curtis Butler a joke? Do we really have Nazis in our school? Somebody say it ain't so! I can't believe what I read!
> —Emma Cortez, sophomore

How far back can this dude trace
his ancestors? Does he realize that
the first humans originated in
Africa?

—Jack Berg, senior

How did that diatribe by Curtis
Butler get front-page space in our
newspaper? We don't need racists
in this school. I threw the issue in
the trash, where it belongs.

—Sean Farmer, junior

What Curtis said in last week's
paper may have seemed pretty
racist, but I'll bet a lot of people
feel the same way and are afraid
to speak up. When you see people
who aren't citizens getting free
medical care and their kids go to
school while your own family has
to pay every time you go to the
emergency room and pay taxes
and stuff, you get a little pissed.

—Jon Klaybrook, freshman

I can't believe you would print
that article "Standing Up for
the White Race." What are you

trying to do? Start a race war?
—Christy Lavies, senior

You tell it, bro! Just go live in
Germany and take your prejudice
with you.
—Aaron Truitt, junior

Let's have a school debate and
invite Curtis Butler to be on the
panel. Here's a question for
starters: Since all the explorers
who discovered America were
men, should only men have rights
of citizenship in this country?
—Zachary Murdo, senior

Hitler was right, but history got it
wrong. If he really had managed
to weed out the misfits and create
a superrace of strong people
with superior minds, the world
wouldn't be having the problems
we have today.
—Eric Haller, sophomore

If we really want to be fair and
just, the United States should

belong to the Native American
tribes who were here first, and the
rest of us should get the heck out.
—Jacob Early, senior

Congratulations to *The Edge* for
printing what will undoubtedly
cause a lot of flak, but hopefully
a lot of good discussion. Keep it
coming. That's where our paper
gets its name.
—Shauna Perkins, senior

The security guards were very visible the day
this latest issue came out, the last day of school
before Christmas vacation. Some of the GSA
members wore their rainbow armbands to show
their solidarity. A few guys and one girl painted
double eights on their foreheads, and there was
a shoving match near the gym, but it was broken
up in a hurry, not by security, but by students
themselves.

The newspaper staff was nervous, I'll admit.
Beck and Gephardt had only halfheartedly
endorsed our approach at the start, but once the
racist views in our school rose to the surface where
we could now touch them, the administration

seemed to think the newspaper coverage might help turn things around.

I was miserable regardless. My throbbing head and stuffed-up nose used up my energy. I knew that with all the tension of the last couple of weeks, my resistance was low, but why did I have to have a cold at Christmas?

One good thing happened, though. Mr. Beck paid a visit to the newsroom.

"However this plays out, I think you've done the school a service," he told us. "This is only the beginning of a dialogue we need to get started in this school. We're thinking of organizing a periodic 'talk-out' in January, where we divide students in groups of ten, with a moderator, and everyone can express their feelings as long as they can do it with respect and consideration for all points of view."

"Fingers crossed," said Phil.

Patrick called me that night.

"Just got in," he said. "I've been doing research for one of the poli-sci profs, and he wanted me to stay one more day. I told him there's a certain girl I have to see. Can I come over?"

"Of course!" I said. "But I've got a cold!"

"You sound like it," he said. "In fact, you sound really awful."

"It's been coming on for a week. Just all the

uproar at school. I don't want you to catch it."

"It wouldn't matter if you had the plague. I'm coming," he said.

We hugged there in the hallway. I tried to keep my germs away from him, but it was difficult. He kissed my forehead, not my mouth, and seemed to be even taller than he'd been when I visited him in July.

"Of all times for me to be sick, Patrick!" I wailed. "I've waited for this for so long."

"Remember the time I got sick and couldn't take you to the eighth-grade semi-formal?" Patrick reminded me. "You were pretty understanding then, if I remember correctly."

"But I didn't love you half as much then," I whispered. Was this the first time I'd actually said *love*?

"Then let's just enjoy now," he said, and held me tight.

"Maybe your mom will change her mind about leaving and will talk your dad into staying here another few years," I said hopefully into the collar of his shirt. A really stupid comment. The movers were coming in—what?—five days.

"No. They've made up their minds. I'm just supposed to see them through it." He held me even closer. "It would be different if I were still in high school, Dad said. But I'm there at the university, about an hour from my uncle's."

"Can we get together with the gang while you're home?" I asked. "Are you going to tell them good-bye?"

"It's not like I'm saying good-bye, Alice. I'll be coming back for your prom. You'll be coming to visit me. You've got an aunt in Chicago." He held me away from him for a moment and shook me gently. "You worry too much."

"And you don't worry enough," I told him. "A lot can happen when two people are apart."

"A lot can happen when they're together," he said. "Look at Jill and Justin. They broke up."

"They're back together," I said.

"So there you have it!" he joked as I guided him to the family room.

We spent part of Christmas Eve with each other. Patrick was here for dinner and helped me wrap some last-minute gifts for my family because I was continually holding a tissue to my nose. My head felt as heavy as a pumpkin, and either my nose was running like a faucet or it was stopped up and I had to breathe through my mouth.

"I don't want you to catch this!" I insisted. "You'll be miserable if you have to fly back with a cold. You *are* flying, aren't you?"

"Yeah. I have to go back on the twenty-seventh, but Mom and Dad will leave in the car as soon as the movers are gone the next day. I'll be working for this professor all through winter break. He's paying minimum wage."

"What's he doing that's so special?"

"He'll be teaching a course in Spain next year, part of a foreign studies class for upperclassmen. Wants to have his lesson plans all done before June."

"And you're an expert on Spain?"

"Hey, I'm an expert on everything," Patrick joked, and kissed the back of my neck, about the only safe spot.

We opened our gifts to each other. Patrick gave me a gorgeous scarf of lamb's wool, soft as a breeze, in graduated shades of green.

"It's beautiful!" I said, holding it out at arm's length, afraid I'd drip on it.

I guess we both had the same theme in mind—something to keep the other warm when we couldn't be together—because I gave him a gray sweater with narrow black stripes.

When he left later to go to a midnight service with his parents, I lay in bed, Kleenex stuffed in one nostril, a box of Tylenol PM on my night stand, and wondered what Fate had against me that I'd had to wait three months to see my boyfriend and then couldn't even kiss him properly.

• • •

We spent Christmas Day alone with our families, and Christmas night with the gang over at the Stedmeisters; we'd told Mark's mom we were stopping by, and she begged us to stay for supper, so we did. Eleven of us crowded into their living room, some bringing tree ornaments with Mark's name on them, some of us with brownies or Christmas cookies, and I could tell how pleased his parents were that we had come. I tried to sit apart from the others so I wouldn't infect anyone.

Mr. Stedmeister showed us Mark's room, which he had turned into a photo gallery almost, having framed about every photo he'd taken of his son. Moving left to right, you could follow Mark from the day he came home from the hospital, up through his toddler years, Cub Scouts, his first dance, first car. . . .

"God, I miss him," his dad said as we neared the end of the photos, and there was a tremor in his voice. "But he'll always be a part of this house, this family."

Just like the Fourth of July, when rain had kept us from going to the fireworks celebration, we hunkered down on their living room rug to watch a Christmas special at the Kennedy Center on TV, the Stedmeisters moving in and out of the room with leftover turkey and ham, homemade mincemeat pie and coconut cake, each of us having pigged out already at Christmas dinners with our own families.

Brian Brewster, in what had to be the most insensitive gesture of the evening, came by in the new yellow Toyota his dad had bought for him now that his license had been restored and invited us to come outside to admire it. As though Mark's accident had never happened. As though the Stedmeisters didn't have to live with the knowledge that their son reached the end of his life crushed between an SUV and a delivery truck.

"Brian . . . ," I said, as he stood just inside the door, beaming and jiggling his car keys.

And it suddenly took.

"Hey, I'm sorry," he said, shoving the keys back in his pocket and coming on in. "Sometimes I get carried away. Merry Christmas, everybody. How's it going?"

Mrs. Stedmeister offered him a plate. "Just help yourself to what's on the table there," she said. "It's so nice to see you, Brian."

Patrick spent his last night, the twenty-sixth, with me. Not the *whole* night. Not even a whole evening. My nose wasn't running quite as much, but it was still red and sore. Dad and Sylvia came in to chat awhile, then left the family room and the fire to us. But we heard Dad rummaging around in the kitchen a few times, and Sylvia went into the office next to the dining room to get something. We put our feet on a hassock and let the fire warm our legs, my head on Patrick's shoulder, his arms pulling me close.

"How am I going to get through the next semester without seeing you once?" I asked. "It's a long time until May."

"It won't be easy for me either," he said.

"Patrick, *everything* is easy for you!" I protested.

I could feel his body stiffen. "We've had this conversation before, Alice. You know it's not."

I was instantly sorry. "You're right. I want a perfect life, I guess. I want you here, not in Chicago. And if I can't have you here full-time, I want you back for vacations. And if I can't have you back for vacations, I want . . . I don't know. To stow away in your suitcase and let you smuggle me back to your dorm."

He nuzzled my hair. "To sleep in my dorm room with Jonah and me?"

I sighed. "There's always a spoiler, isn't there?"

We talked a long time about what had gone on at school—about Curtis Butler and his white-power views; about Dennis Granger, now that his case had gone public; about the Stedmeisters and Molly and Keeno and Brian—and finally we took the lap robes Sylvia keeps around the family room and tiptoed out onto the back porch, where the two-seater glider rocked slightly in the wind.

The cushions were dusty and cold, but we put one of the lap robes beneath us, and in time the warmth of the robes and the heat of our own bodies replaced the chill. We clung to each other.

"I wish . . . we could have each other," Patrick whispered in my ear.

My heart was racing. "So do I," I whispered back. "But this isn't a good place."

"I know. Just wishing," he said, and stroked my breasts.

"Patrick," I said, my head against his chest. "When we do . . . I don't want it to be a one-time thing. . . ."

"A one-night stand? Why do you think it would be?"

"I mean, I want it to be the best place, the best time . . . when we could have each other again and again. I don't want you going off somewhere when . . . things . . . are still sort of . . . new."

"Okay."

I pulled away from him. "You understand?"

"I think so." He pulled me down on his chest again. "But . . . God! I do want you."

I guided his hand beneath my sweater, and wordlessly, we unbuttoned buttons, unzipped zippers, and explored each other's bodies under the blankets, listening to the sound of our breathing and our pleasure in each other.

Three days after Christmas, the same day the moving van came and the Longs left for their new home in Wisconsin, I got early acceptance from the University of Maryland.

"Yay!" I said, opening the envelope there in the kitchen where Dad and Sylvia were making kebabs for dinner. "I'm in! You won't have to mortgage the house!"

"Well, that's good to know!" Dad said. "I didn't think you'd be hearing from colleges so soon, Al. You applied for early acceptance? This doesn't obligate you to go there, does it?"

"No, but it means I'm pretty serious about it."

"Well, let's don't make a final decision until you've heard from the others," Dad said. "You might like being farther away—a whole new community to explore."

"Or not," I said. "If one of you got sick . . . or the store closed . . . I could live at home and commute, and it would save you a bundle."

"Al, you're not going to choose a college on a bunch of what-ifs. I want you to go to the college of your choice. But if you decide on the University of Maryland, you've got to live in a dorm. I'm willing to buy you a used car when it's time so you can get home now and then, but you have to live there during the school year. That's a must."

"I . . . have to?"

"That's my condition. You've got to have the experience of living independently, learning to trust yourself, getting along with roommates . . . That's as much a part of college as the courses."

I silently began setting the table for dinner. The thought of having a car helped considerably. Still . . . were they kicking me out? Had they been waiting for the chance to have the house to themselves for so long that all they could think of was having me gone? What if Patrick . . . ?

And suddenly I realized that if I was living in a dorm, Patrick could visit me *there*. I could arrange for my roommate to be out for the evening. *I* could smuggle him into *my* bed. We wouldn't have to sit out on a cold glider on a freezing porch in December. We wouldn't have to talk in a family room with parents close by. And it didn't matter which college I chose, I could still invite Patrick.

"Okay," I said with finality. "If I choose Maryland, I'll live in a dorm."

22

To Life

On the twenty-ninth I was feeling well enough to make a short visit to the mall. I had just used a gift card from Aunt Sally when I almost bumped into Curtis Butler. He was coming out of a Sports Authority store, bag in hand.

"Hey, Curtis!" I said, backing up to avoid a collision.

"Hey," he said, looking at me uncertainly. "How ya doin'?"

I think he was going to walk on by, but because I stopped, he did. It was awkward.

"How was Christmas?" I asked.

"It was okay. How about yours?"

"Nice. My brother graduated from Maryland, so it was sort of special," I told him.

"I guess." He looked about hesitantly, took a few steps toward the escalator, then stopped and came back. "Listen. I just wanted you to know that some of that stuff—and a couple of letters—I didn't do. Sometimes the other guys get carried away."

"Okay," I said. "Glad you told me."

We fell silent again. I nodded toward the ice-cream tables in one of the side corridors. "Want to sit down for a minute? I've got some questions."

He shrugged. We walked over to a table, and he put his bag on it. Shoes, I guessed. He sat perched on the edge of his chair as if to say, *A minute's all I've got.*

"*The Edge* has been getting a lot of letters since we published your piece, and one of them, as you probably know, suggested a debate. The newspaper would be glad to sponsor it." *Here I go again*, I thought, *climbing out on a limb all by myself.*

"We're . . . really not into that," Curtis said.

I·studied him. "Who's *we*, exactly?"

He looked away. "Different groups. Different names."

"Do you consider yourselves racist?"

"Yeah, I suppose so. In a good sense."

"Good how?"

"We're not saying that other races shouldn't exist. I'm not, anyway. We're just saying that the white race has been getting a bum rap, and it's time we took the country back, that's all."

"You want some ice cream while we're sitting here?" I asked, hoping to prolong things. "I'm buying."

"No, thanks. I gotta get going."

"I just wanted to tell you that after I read your essay for the paper, I realized it sounded as though you'd memorized some of those hate group sites on the Web."

He shrugged again. "They say it better, that's all." And then he added, "But . . . after I read some of those responses in *The Edge*, I asked Vance—"

"Vance?"

"He's twenty. Sort of in charge of our unit. I asked him if he'd give a talk . . . anything . . . at school. I mean, now that we've got an opening. . . ."

"He agreed?"

Curtis shook his head. "He said we don't get mixed up in that. We are what we are."

I didn't say anything. Curtis shifted uneasily, then leaned forward, resting his arms on his knees. "Well, that sort of got to me, know what I mean? You let me write that essay, and I put myself on the line. I'll pick up a lot of crap. And now that we've got a chance, Vance says no."

"Did he say why?"

"He says they always try to trick you, and when we're right, we're right, and you don't have to explain it."

I smiled. "That's what they told Galileo when he insisted the earth revolved around the sun."

Curtis didn't return the smile. "Well, I'm just saying that I've sort of been thinking this over, and I figure if we believe it, we should be able to defend it."

"You could always debate it on your own. Get some of your friends to be on the panel too." I could only imagine how this would go over.

"I don't know that I'm ready for that yet," he said. "I just joined last summer. Anyway, Vance sort of nixed the idea. His solution is that everybody should get a free ticket back to where he came from. Keep it simple. It'll never happen, but it should."

"Then we'd *all* disappear."

He shrugged my comment off as though it weren't worth arguing about.

"Curtis, did you ever get to know—really know—someone from another race? Another country? Make a real friend, I mean?"

"Hey, I don't need to *know* the bean eater's family. I don't need to *know* the blacks who got the jobs we could have had. I know what they got, and that's enough." Curtis turned away again, his face angry.

"Did you ever think that the United States is the only home most people here have ever known?"

"Not our boy from Sudan."

"No. Africa's his country and eventually, he *is* going back. He's here to see how the real America works."

Curtis didn't answer for a moment. Then he said, "Okay, so his village was burned down. I didn't do it. The U.S. didn't do it. But here they are in this country, getting all the breaks."

"Some people risked their lives to get here," I said.

"So? The answer isn't to give them what's meant for red-blooded Americans either, that's for damn sure." He shook his head. "I don't know. Some of the things the guys are doing . . . I don't see it. 'For the cause,' they say."

"And the cause is . . . ?"

"Helping the white race see blacks and Hispanics for what they are."

"I don't see any of it, frankly. I don't know where all that hate comes from."

He went on talking as though he hadn't heard me. "Vance says my heart isn't one hundred percent in it. He wants to try our operation in a different school."

"Scare tactics? Is that what you're telling me?" I asked.

I could sense that Curtis was ending the conversation. "I'm not telling you anything. I'm just saying that's how some groups operate. To each his own. Vance can do without me? Fine. I'll find a group I like better. But, anyway . . . I do my job, you do yours. You're features editor, aren't you?"

"Yeah. By the skin of my teeth. I've made some mistakes this year."

"Like asking me to write that article?"

I gave him a questioning smile. "Guess we'll have to see how this one plays out. We've got a dialogue going—in print, at least—and that's good."

"Yeah. Well . . ." He stood up and picked up his bag. "I gotta go. See you around."

"See you," I said.

It was only two days later that I saw Curtis again.

In return for Sylvia's help with altering our dresses for the Snow Ball, I told her I'd fill her gas tank and pay for it this time—wash the windshield and check the tires, too, a job she hates.

I put a hoodie on over my sweater, pulled on a pair of gloves, and drove to the gas station. Other drivers were there, filling their tanks for their New Year's Eve destinations before the storm that was to blow in that night. Hard to believe when the air seemed unusually warm for December and the sun was out. But a cold gray mass was coming in over the horizon, and I figured that Fate, which had assigned me a cold over Christmas, was planning to ruin New Year's Eve for a lot of people too.

After I filled the tank, I moved the car over

to the air hose and began checking each tire. I noticed Curtis and two older men standing next to a pickup truck outside the service bay area of the garage. They were joking around about something, and a mechanic came out to talk with them. Curtis strongly resembled both men— same deep-set eyes, same shape of the jaw, same build—father and uncle, I guessed.

I was crouched down on one side of the car with the tire gauge, in no hurry to stand up as I watched the tableau unfold. Curtis was evidently the butt of some joke, because one of the men took little not-so-playful jabs at his stomach to punctuate a point.

"Cut it out, Dad," Curtis said at last, his face a dull shade of pink.

His father laughed and said to the mechanic, "Thinks he's going to join the Marines."

"That a fact?" the mechanic said, pulling a rag from a back pocket and wiping the grease from his hands.

"He doesn't drive an ATV better'n he drives that Chevy in there, he's gonna make one sorry-ass Marine," said the uncle.

"Make a better Marine than you would," Curtis said.

With lightning speed, his father kicked one foot out from under him, and Curtis tottered, almost falling to the ground. He righted himself just in time and now his face was crimson. Both men laughed.

"Why the hell you do that?" Curtis said hotly.

His dad was still laughing and drew up his fists. "Wanna fight? Wanna fight?" He threw a fake punch at Curtis's jaw.

"Hey, son," the mechanic said. "Come on in here and let me show you what we did for the Chevy."

"Never could take a joke," the dad said as Curtis sullenly followed the mechanic inside.

"Toughen up the little shit, make a man out of him before he can be a Marine," said the uncle.

I checked the pressure of the fourth tire, slowly hung up the air hose, and drove away.

Patrick called me from Chicago that evening. The cold rain that had come in during the afternoon was already turning to ice in our area, and people were staying off the roads. You couldn't even get to a neighbor's without falling down, so people were advised to stay home. We were texting like mad and calling all over the place. But it was Patrick's call I'd been waiting for.

"So how are you spending the evening if you can't go out?" he asked. "I'm going to a triple feature at Ida Noyes Hall. I'll probably fizzle out after watching two films back-to-back."

"I'm writing the article in memory of Mark that I promised myself I'd do last September," I said. "It keeps morphing into something else, and I'm not sure of where it's going, but I'm giving it a try."

"I'm glad we visited the Stedmeisters on Christmas. Did you get the feeling Mark's mom was just waiting for a crowd to come? That somehow she knew we'd show?"

"Yeah," I said. "I kept thinking, what would she have done with all that food if nobody came?"

I'd already e-mailed Patrick that I'd been accepted at the U of Maryland next year, and we talked about the two other colleges and about how Patrick was liking their new house.

"Funny, but my dorm room seems more like home to me than the house," Patrick said. "I don't know the new neighborhood. Don't know any of the people, don't know the yard, the street, the trees. . . . I was thinking about that last night: how maybe the new house will always be my parents' house, not mine; that home for me, from now on, will be wherever my stuff is. Weird."

"I wonder if I'll ever feel the same way," I said. "Is it . . . have you ever felt homesick when you were away? Missed your folks, I mean? Or have you traveled so much that living out of a suitcase is old hat?"

"I was homesick a couple of times when I

went to camp, but that's all. I guess I see life more as an adventure. Always wondering where I'll be a year from now. What I'll be doing."

For me, I thought, I was getting to a place that wherever Patrick was, that's where I wanted to be.

I had been delaying the writing of Mark's memorial tribute because there was both too little and too much to say. When September became October, and that turned to November, I'd put it off once again, thinking I'd write the piece and, after it was published, slip it in a Christmas card to Mr. and Mrs. Stedmeister. Now Christmas was over, and here it was, New Year's.

Mark was a good friend—not a close personal friend who confided in me, but a "group friend" I'd watched grow up ever since I met him in sixth grade.

The summer after, I'd been there when he became Pamela's first boyfriend. I was with Pamela when he and Brian stuck gum in her hair and she had to cut it. As one of the best-looking guys in seventh grade, he was dubbed one of the "Three Handsome Stooges," and we commiserated with him in eighth grade when, in a Critical Choices class, the "problem" he was assigned to solve was how—working two jobs and with no college education—he could possibly provide child support for eighteen years to a "baby he had fathered with his girlfriend."

By tenth grade the Stedmeisters' pool was the gathering place for our crowd on Monday nights during the summer. We worried about Mark when he fell too much under Brian's influence, then watched him become more self-confident as he and Keeno worked on old cars.

Though Mark was never particularly outstanding in any accomplishment, he was a necessary part of our scene. If he was missing, we were incomplete, but I couldn't say why.

I was thinking about the uniqueness of stars. I was thinking about snowflakes. And then my mind drifted back to the discussion we'd had at church about the odds that any of us had been born at all, and I sat down at my computer to write.

IN MEMORIAM

Mark Stedmeister would have described himself as a "regular Joe." I never knew him to volunteer for a special project, because he didn't think his abilities were special. If you asked for his help, however, he was right there. He was on the quiet side—didn't often tell jokes or stories—but in our crowd Mark was as essential as air.

Sure, he was one of the first guys to own a car and he drove us around. When he wasn't going out with a girl, he was always available to make up a foursome. But it was his presence we needed to make us complete. When one of us told a joke, he was right with us, all the way, his eyes bright with anticipation from the start. We watched those familiar laugh lines deepen on his face as we approached the punch line, and he was the first to throw back his head and let out the series of chuckles that became his trademark. If we had a story to tell, he'd settle back and grin like he'd paid good money for our entertainment and knew it would be good.

Summers we met weekly, sometimes more, at the Stedmeisters' pool, horsing around, eating his mom's food, often leaving our wet towels in their bathroom, treating their place like our own. He never said we were a pain, never asked us to leave, never complained when he carried in all our glasses and plates and scraps of pizza when we forgot our manners and didn't offer to help. If Mark couldn't make one of our parties, we felt it. If his laughter was missing, jokes weren't the same.

I'd met Mark in sixth grade and figured he'd be part of our lives as long as we went to this school. As long as we lived in this neighborhood. We danced with him, swam with him, argued with him, studied with him, and finally, mourned for him when he was killed in a car accident last August.

We missed him at homecoming in September. He would have worn some crazy getup at Halloween. Over the Thanksgiving holidays we would have gotten together, and when we stopped by his house this Christmas, only his parents were there.